SAVING MISSISSIPPI

Cornelia Funke

First published in Great Britain
in 2010 by The Chicken House
This Large Print edition published by
AudioGO Ltd 2011
by arrangement with
The Chicken House

ISBN 978 1405 664738

First published in Germany as
Hande Weg Mississippi
Original text copyright © 1997
Cecilie Dressler Verlag,
Hamburg, Germany
English translation by Anthea Bell
copyright © 2010 Cornelia Funke
Cornelia Funke has asserted her right
under the Copyright, Designs and
Patents Act, 1988, to be identified as
the author of this work

British Library Cataloguing Publication Data available

Printed and bound in Great Britain by
CPI Antony Rowe, Chippenham and Eastbourne

For Tena, Lena and Inga

CHAPTER 1

As Emma got off the bus, she closed her eyes and took a deep breath.

Oh yes! This was how it ought to smell. Of manure, petrol and damp earth.

Of summer holidays with Dolly.

*   *   *

Emma happily turned off her mobile phone; blissfully there had never been any mobile reception in this village! She flung her rucksack on to her back and hopped across the road. She spat in the village pond, jumped into two puddles, and then she was at her grandmother's garden gate. Everything was the same as ever.

The paint was peeling off the old house, and instead of geraniums there was lettuce growing in Dolly's window boxes. The car had another dent in it, and Emma hadn't met the black cat sitting on the dustbin before. But the wobbly garden table under the walnut tree was laid to welcome her, just as usual. Chickens were stalking around on the grass, and Dolly's old dogs Tom and Jerry lay asleep outside the open front door. They didn't even lift their noses when Emma pushed open the gate and ran towards the house. Only when she was right in front of them did they wag their tails sleepily and put their muddy paws on her shoes.

'Hi, you super-watchdogs!' Emma tickled them both behind the ears and gave them a few dog biscuits. She always took care to stuff her pockets with those when she was going to see her grandmother.

A burning smell drifted out of the house.

Emma grinned. Dolly must have been trying to do some baking again. She was probably the only grandmother in the world who couldn't manage to bake a cake. She couldn't cook very well either. She did none of the things that Emma's friends' grannies liked doing. Dolly didn't crochet, she didn't knit, she didn't read stories aloud, and every year she forgot Emma's birthday. Her grey hair was cut as short as matchsticks, she usually wore men's clothes, and she repaired her car herself.

But Emma wouldn't have swapped her for any other grandmother. 'Hi!' she called into the smoke-filled kitchen. 'I'm back!'

An enormous dog shot out barking from under the kitchen table, jumped up at Emma and licked her face.

'Hello, sweetheart.' Dolly was crouching in front of the oven, looking quite unhappy. She took her cake out and slammed it on to the kitchen table. 'Just look at that! Too brown. Again! I can't understand it. I even got myself one of those stupid kitchen timers.'

The enormous dog left Emma alone and sniffed the burnt cake.

'Good thing I bought some shop cake, just to be on the safe side.' Dolly wiped her floury hands on her trousers and gave Emma a kiss. 'So nice that you're back! I hope you missed me!'

'You bet.' Emma took her rucksack off and held a few dog biscuits in front of the new dog's muzzle. 'And where did this one come from?'

'Shaggy?' Dolly took a large packet of cake out of the kitchen cupboard and went outside with Emma in tow. 'Mr Knapp, the vet, found him on the motorway slip road. You know how dogs like that always end up with me.'

Emma smiled.

She certainly did know! Hens that didn't lay eggs, pregnant cats, dogs who chewed up rugs—her grandmother took them all in. She even had an old gelding in the paddock behind the house. His name was Aldo. Dolly had saved him from the knacker's yard four years ago, and taught Emma how to ride him.

'How's Aldo?' Emma asked.

Dolly sat down on the garden seat that Emma's grandpa had made many years ago, and poured her a mug of cocoa. 'Aldo? He's fine. A bit of trouble with his teeth, but he still tries to eat me out of house and home.'

'What else?' Emma took a piece of cake. A chicken disappeared under the table and pecked at her shoelace.

4

'You can hear what else.'

The sound of a spluttering engine came from Mr Procter's car repair shop next door, and Dolly's other neighbour, Lizzie Dockfoot, was sweeping the path in front of her garden wall to the soundtrack of her radio.

'Hey, Lizzie!' called Dolly. 'Could you turn your radio down a bit? All that racket's making my coffee spill over.'

Muttering to herself, Lizzie shuffled to the garden wall, turned off the radio and came over to Dolly's fence.

'Here.' She threw an empty cigarette packet and two lolly sticks over. 'I found these on my side of your fence.'

'Oh, you're welcome to keep them,' said Dolly. 'Like a coffee, Lizzie?'

'No, thank you.' Lizzie Dockfoot nodded to Emma. 'Hello, Emma, I thought you'd gone home.'

'I did.' Emma suppressed a giggle. 'But that was three months ago, Mrs Dockfoot. It's the summer holidays now.'

'Yes?' Lizzie Dockfoot bent down

5

and pulled out a couple of weeds growing by Dolly's fence. 'Dandelions, horrid stuff. Enjoy your cake, you two, some of us have work to do.'

Making a sour face, she reached for her broom, cranked up the radio again, and went on sweeping.

Dolly sighed, but Emma couldn't help grinning. 'Everything's just the same,' she said. 'Wonderful!'

At home, everything was changing yet again. While Emma was staying with Dolly her parents were moving into their new flat. New flat, new town, new school. Emma didn't want to think about it.

'Just the same?' Dolly shook her head. 'Not quite, sweetheart. Old Clipperbush died last week.'

'Oh dear!' Emma looked at her grandmother in shock. 'He wasn't *that* old.'

Dolly shook her head. 'Not much older than me. But I'm sure you're going to hear all about it any moment now,' she added, pointing to the gate. 'Look who's here. Word that you're back gets around pretty fast.'

Two boys came running round the village pond. Leo and Max were the sons of the baker opposite. They raced each other to Dolly's garden gate. Max vaulted over it first, as usual. He put his tongue out at his brother and sprinted for the empty chair beside Emma. Leo, looking annoyed, followed him. 'You pushed me!' he hissed at his brother. 'Just to show off to Emma!'

'Now, now, you two!' Dolly lifted up her cup. 'You almost spilt my coffee with all your pushing and shoving. Want something to drink? Or a piece of cake?'

'Did you bake it yourself?' asked Max suspiciously.

'What's that supposed to mean?'

'If you didn't, then yes please.'

'The cheek!' said Dolly, standing up. 'But I'll get you both some juice anyway.'

She went back to the house, followed by Shaggy.

'Hi, Emma,' Leo murmured.

'Hey, did you hear what happened?' Max pushed his brother out of the way. 'Old Mr Clipperbush fell down dead

7

outside our shop. Just like that. Slam!—and there he was, flat on his back. You remember old Clipperbush, don't you?'

Emma nodded. She remembered him very well. Every Sunday he would ride through the village on his mare, Mississippi. He would weave coloured ribbons into her mane, with little bells on them. Clipperbush himself always wore a real Stetson cowboy hat, and every time he rode past Dolly he used to take it off and wave it to her.

'Dead as a headless chicken, he was,' said Max.

Leo helped himself to a piece of cake, sat down where Dolly had been sitting and drank some of her milky coffee.

'Did you—I mean,' said Emma, looking at the two of them uncomfortably, 'did you see it happen?'

'You bet we did,' said Max. 'Well, I did. This one here,' he added, nudging his brother, 'went straight round behind the house and puked.'

'I did not,' said Leo.

'You did so,' said Max, almost

8

shoving his brother off his chair. 'I wanted to hold a mirror in front of Clipperbush's mouth, like they always do in films, but Mum wouldn't let me. His horse got terribly upset. As if she knew what had happened. No one but Mr Knapp could calm her down.'

Emma knew Mr Knapp the vet as well. He was a regular visitor to Dolly's house. Something was always wrong with one or other of her animals.

'Well,' said Dolly, coming back with a bottle of juice, 'I suppose these two have told you all about poor Clipperbush's passing?'

'So what if we did?' muttered Max. 'I mean, you don't see a person fall down dead every day.'

'Luckily,' said Dolly. 'I'm going to miss Clipperbush. But he had a good death.'

'Dad says he was crazy,' remarked Max.

'I dare say.' Dolly put a piece of cake on her saucer and handed it to him. 'Your father thinks half the village is crazy. Me too, I'm sure.'

'But what happened to his mare?'

9

asked Emma.

The boys shrugged.

'That horse is definitely crazy,' Max observed with his mouth full.

Thoughtfully, Dolly smoothed out the tablecloth. 'Knapp is looking after her for now. But Clipperbush's nephew will probably inherit everything, and no doubt he'll sell the mare.'

'What a pity,' murmured Emma.

Mr Clipperbush used to smarten Mississippi up in a slightly different way every time he went out riding on her. Emma and Dolly had sometimes laid bets on whether the mare would have flowers behind her ears today or little bells on her reins. Every Sunday they used to sit in suspense under the walnut tree, waiting to see who had won the bet.

And when Clipperbush did ride by, he used to wave his hat and call, 'Good morning, ladies.'

Yes, Emma would miss him too.

She certainly would.

CHAPTER 2

When Emma's alarm clock went off at six the next morning Dolly was already out. She delivered newspapers five days a week, riding her bike around her own village and two others nearby.

Emma splashed her face with cold water, ate a slice of toast and marmalade without sitting down—and got to work herself.

Seven cats rubbed round her legs, and the dogs were creating quite a racket, impatiently pushing their food bowls about on the flagstones. When Dolly was on her own, she fed all the animals before starting on her newspaper round.

'Bad luck, you lot,' said Emma, looking for the can opener in the cutlery drawer. 'For the next six weeks you don't get anything until I fall out of bed.'

By the time she had opened all the cat-food cans, her fingers hurt as if someone had been chewing them. Luckily the dogs ate dried food!

Next came the birds: the three budgies in the living room, and then the chickens—they all needed fresh water and lots of seeds. Then Emma fed the two old goats. And finally, she went to see to Aldo. She always kept the best for last.

Every morning she looked forward to Aldo nudging her with his nose and searching her jacket pockets for carrots. Then Emma would dream that Aldo was really her horse. A crazy dream! The new flat that her parents were moving into was on the fourth floor again, because if they lived as high up as that then Emma's mother wasn't so scared of burglars. Emma wouldn't even be able to keep a guinea pig there. So it was downright ridiculous to dream of having her own horse. But all the same, Emma caught herself dreaming that dream again and again. Especially when she was stroking Aldo's soft nose.

Every time she came to visit, Emma wondered whether the old gelding had forgotten her. She spent as much time as possible at Dolly's house, but all the same, there were weeks and weeks in between the holidays.

'Hi, Aldo,' she said as she went into the stable. 'Hungry?'

The horse raised his head and whickered. Emma lovingly petted him and blew gently into his nostrils. That was how horses said hello to each other, she had once read. Emma read a lot of books about horses. Far too many of them, her mother thought.

Aldo snorted back. So hard that Emma gasped for air, giggling. The horse's breath made her feel quite dizzy. She filled Aldo's manger and brought him fresh water. Dolly was always reminding her that that was more important than anything else. Horses hated to drink stagnant or dirty water. They'd rather not drink anything at all, and that could be very dangerous, because then they could get colic. When Aldo had munched his hay and had a drink, Emma took him into the paddock. She had already tethered the goats to their stakes. If those two weren't tied up, they'd jump any fence. They weren't exactly the best of company for a horse, but better than nothing.

'Horses turn peculiar if they're on their own too much,' Dolly always said. 'Just like people.'

By the time Emma had swept out the stable and collected the eggs from the hens' nests, she felt so tired that she could happily have gone straight back to bed.

Her first day at Dolly's was always like that.

But of course Emma didn't go back to bed. Yawning, she went into the kitchen to make breakfast. Then she remembered that she'd forgotten to feed the fish again. She was always forgetting them, because she didn't like fish much. Neither did Dolly, but she always said that wasn't the fishes' fault, and of course she was right.

When Dolly came home, Emma was asleep on the sofa in the kitchen. But breakfast was ready—soft-boiled eggs, a Thermos jug of strong coffee, cocoa and fresh rolls. Emma had fetched the rolls from Leo and Max's father on the other side of the village pond.

It took Dolly some time to tickle her awake again. 'Well?' she said. 'Country air making you tired already, is it?'

'Terribly tired!' muttered Emma, sitting up sleepily. 'How can you be so wide awake at this time of day?'

'Ah, well,' said Dolly, sighing as she sat down at the kitchen table, 'I don't mind getting up early. You need less sleep at my age, anyway, but all this cycling about . . . awful! I have to do three villages these days. I'm sometimes so tempted to take the car.'

'Shall I deliver the papers for you?' asked Emma. 'I wouldn't mind that at all.'

'No, don't do that,' Dolly laughed, 'or I'll never get back on my bike when you go home again.'

'Can't you just give the job up?' asked Emma. 'I mean, you have your pension, and you inherited a bit from Grandpa.'

'Well,' Dolly took a sip of coffee, 'Aldo isn't getting any younger, the

15

dogs need their vaccinations, and one or other of the cats is always having kittens. That adds up to a lot of vet's bills, and I can use every penny.'

Emma nodded.

At that moment there was a knock at the door.

Tom and Jerry stayed where they were, but Shaggy shot out from under the table so fast that Emma spilt cocoa over her jeans.

Before Dolly could reach the door, Shaggy had already pushed the handle down.

'Out of the way, you daft dog,' said Dolly, squeezing laboriously past the tail-wagging giant of an animal.

Aaron Knapp the vet was standing outside.

When Shaggy saw him, he quickly disappeared under the table again.

'Well, talk of the devil!' said Dolly. 'What are you doing here? Did I call you?'

'No!' said the vet. 'Dammit, Dolly, I'm so furious I could explode!'

Mr Knapp had to duck his head so as not to bump it on Dolly's doorway.

Crossly, he stomped past her into the kitchen. When he saw Emma, he managed a little smile. 'Oh, hi, Emma, back here in the country again?'

'Good heavens!' Dolly pushed a chair over to him. 'You're as red as a beetroot. What's the matter?'

Mr Knapp put his vet's bag down and tried folding his long, long legs under the table, but there simply wasn't room for them among the noses of all those dogs.

'Would you like some coffee?' asked Emma.

'What? Oh yes, please.' The vet took off his glasses and cleaned them.

'Well, come on, spit it out!' Dolly shooed a cat off her chair and sat down again. 'Who's put you in such a temper?'

Knapp smoothed down his untidy hair. 'You know I go out to Clipperbush's farm every morning,' said the vet, 'because I'm looking after his mare—she's all on her own in her stable now. For days I've been waiting for his nephew to come and look at the farm and decide what's to happen to

17

the animal. He's probably the heir to the property, if he's the old man's only living relative.'

'That's how I see it myself,' Dolly agreed. 'Clipperbush didn't particularly like him, but he's his favourite sister's son.'

'He's a nasty piece of work!' said the vet. 'Do you know what he said to me this morning when I finally found him in the farmyard?' Knapp slammed his hand down on the table so hard that Emma's cocoa slopped over. 'He told me he'd already phoned the abattoir! Well, so there you are!'

Dolly shook her head. 'Sounds just like Clipperbush's nephew,' she said. 'I met him at the old man's place a few times, and that was quite enough. His name's Albert, isn't it?'

The vet nodded. 'Albert Gosling. And guess what?' He leaned over the table. 'When I told that young man that the horse is fit as a fiddle, could easily live another ten years, and that he'd better find a place where they'll look after her if he can't do it himself, he grinned in my face and said, "The

18

knacker will give me a couple of hundred quid for her, and anything else will cost me money." That was all he had to say!'

'Drink your coffee,' said Dolly. 'It'll calm you down. Why doesn't he try selling the mare if he's so keen to get his hands on some money? She isn't all that old.'

'Not old, no, but you know what she looks like!' Mr Knapp took a sip of the coffee Emma had made, and shook himself. 'My word, this is strong!'

'Yes, Emma makes good coffee,' said Dolly. 'You can stand the spoon up in it.'

'Mississippi . . .' The vet drank some more coffee, very carefully this time. 'Mississippi may have been a beauty to old Clipperbush, but she's striped like a zebra ever since she got tangled up in that barbed wire. And she has bad teeth because Clipperbush was always feeding her chocolate. No one's going to buy a horse like that. Even that Gosling knows it. No, he'll let the butcher have Mississippi.'

'But he can't!' cried Emma. 'There

must be something we can do to stop it.'

Dolly sighed. 'I don't know what, darling.'

Mr Knapp looked at Dolly over the rim of his cup. 'Couldn't you have a word with him?'

'Oh, so that's why you're here!' said Dolly.

'Please, Dolly!' Mr Knapp gave her his nicest smile. 'Go and see Mr Clipperbush's nephew and offer to look after Mississippi for free. Do it today. That bloody idiot . . .' Here he looked at Emma, embarrassed. 'Excuse my language, Emma, that . . . er, person is in a hurry to get back to town. You wangle the horse out of him. You're brilliant at that kind of thing.'

'Well, I don't know.' Dolly sliced open another roll and spread it thickly with cherry jam. 'Another dog or cat, you know you can always bring one of those here. But another horse? No, I'm sorry, Knapp.' She waved the idea away. 'Aldo's already eating me out of house and home, not to mention your bills.'

20

'But I'd see to the expenses!' cried the vet. 'I'd pay you for all that. And of course my veterinary services would come free as well.' He looked at Dolly with an injured expression. 'It wouldn't be the first time I've been happy to be paid with a few fresh eggs, would it?'

Dolly did not reply. She just sat there, tracing invisible patterns on the table with the tip of her knife.

'Oh, please, Grandmother!' said Emma. 'I'm sure Aldo would like it.'

'So now you're sticking your oar in!' muttered Dolly. 'Grandmother! When Emma calls me that, I'm defeated anyway.' She groaned. 'I bet you that mare won't touch anything but caviar, because Clipperbush spoilt her so badly. But that's not going to be my problem, is it? You'll be paying for everything, Knapp.'

'Word of honour!' The vet was beaming all over his face. 'I knew you'd help me out.'

'Did you now? You can be glad that Emma backed you up. And that I have a soft spot for animals that no one else wants. Fine then. When shall we go

21

and get her?'

Knapp jumped up, so quickly that he bumped his knee on the underside of the table. 'Right this minute! I'll drive you two over.'

"There we go.' Dolly shook her head. 'Look at him, Emma. As crazy as me. He'd even try to save a three-legged cow from the abattoir.'

'Nonsense!' The vet picked up his bag and awkwardly adjusted his glasses. 'After all, Clipperbush and I used to play cards every Tuesday, and I know how fond of Mississippi he was. I owe it to him. And no horse ought to be turned into sausages.'

'I expect a pig would say the same,' said Dolly. Sighing, she got to her feet. 'Very well then, you two. Let's go. Before I change my mind. Watch out, duck your head, Knapp!'

But the vet had already knocked his head against the doorway.

CHAPTER 3

Old Mr Clipperbush had not by any means been the poorest man in the village. His house was the largest for miles around, and you could have fitted all the thirty-five houses in the village on to the land belonging to it. All the same, when he died there was only a single animal left in his stables—Mississippi.

'Why did he have just one horse?' Emma asked, as they drove to Clipperbush's farm.

'He outlived all the others,' said the vet. 'Or sold them.'

'Sold them? What for?' Emma pushed Jerry's muzzle out of her jacket pocket. There'd been no way to stop Tom and Jerry coming with them, so Emma was sitting on the back seat with both the dogs' heads on her lap.

'Oh, because he was going to emigrate again,' replied the vet. 'To America. It was Clipperbush's great dream. Every seven or eight years he

23

used to sell his animals, pack two huge suitcases, say goodbye to everyone—and then he stayed after all! He was doing it again two weeks before his death. He sold his chickens, cattle, horses, even some of his furniture. But he never could part with Mississippi. He didn't think anyone else was good enough to own her. His suitcases were ready and packed, standing beside his bed. But Mississippi was still here. And then, well, Clipperbush just fell down dead.' The vet stopped at the side of the road. 'I'll drop you two off here. Better if that fellow doesn't see my car. We had something of a shouting match this morning.'

'Really?' Dolly looked at him, shaking her head. 'You didn't tell us everything, then.'

'It was embarrassing!' muttered the vet. 'But the man made me furious. I'll wish you better luck, anyway.'

'Don't worry, it will all work out,' said Dolly. As she got out of the car, Tom and Jerry tried jumping out after her, but Dolly slammed the door in their faces.

'Knapp,' she said, 'we'll leave the dogs with you. Two crazy dogs plus one spoilt mare are too much for my poor nerves. What's more, those two would far rather ride in your car than trot along the road behind us. Bring them back to me later, okay?'

'If you say so.' The vet leaned out of the window. 'Oh, and Dolly,' he whispered. 'Be nice, however badly he behaves. Otherwise he'll do as he said and hand Mississippi over to the knacker just to spite you.'

'Yes, yes!' Dolly grinned. 'People don't upset me so easily.'

'And another thing!' The vet beckoned her closer. 'Here's three hundred pounds. If you can't talk him round, give him the money.'

'You know something, Knapp?' Dolly put the money in her wallet. 'I can't help wondering which of the pair of us will be ruined first by our love of animals. Go on, off with you. It's up to Emma and me now.'

*   *   *

25

Emma thought Clipperbush's house was sinister. Grey and forbidding, it stood at the far end of a paved yard, surrounded by empty sheds and stables and a tall hawthorn hedge. The only way out to the road was through a big iron gate.

'Wouldn't want that house even as a present,' murmured Emma, as Dolly pushed open the gate.

'Clipperbush wasn't specially fond of it either,' said Dolly. 'But it's been in his family for ever and ever, so he never sold it. He didn't even think of selling it when he got that bee in his bonnet about emigrating.'

In silence, they crossed the empty yard. There was nothing there but a big, brand-new car standing outside the stables.

'Does that belong to the nephew?' whispered Emma.

'Why are you whispering?' asked Dolly. 'Afraid old Clipperbush's ghost may hear you? You can bet it'll be in America by now.' She went over to the car and peered through the windows. 'Well, *that* certainly didn't belong to

Clipperbush. Rather flashy for my taste.'

Emma looked around uncomfortably.

The large front door of the house was open just a crack.

'Come on,' said Dolly, and led her towards it. 'It's not so bad inside the house.'

*　　　*　　　*

But Emma thought the house was every bit as gloomy inside.

'Yuk!' she said 'If I had to live in a place like this I'd emigrate myself.'

They found Clipperbush's nephew upstairs in the bedroom. It was the only room that wasn't full of bulky old furniture. Two posters hung on the walls—one of the Grand Canyon and one of a Mississippi steamer. Two packed suitcases stood beside the bed.

When Dolly knocked at the open door, Albert Gosling was closely examining his dead uncle's mattress.

'What are you doing here?' he snapped at Dolly.

Dolly smiled her friendliest smile.

27

'We've come about Mississippi, your late uncle's mare, Mr Gosling. I'm Dolores Flowerdew. Maybe you remember me. We met once or twice here in your uncle's house. I own the farm by the village pond, and you sometimes came wandering around as a child.'

'Oh yes. Of course. The village animal-lover.' Albert Gosling laughed. It wasn't a very nice laugh. 'I remember. Daffy Dolly, that's what my friends and I always called you.'

'Oh, I can remember a few less attractive names as well,' said Dolly. Emma looked at her. Dolly's mouth was smiling, but not her eyes. 'I heard you wanted to get rid of your uncle's mare,' she went on. 'Is that so?'

Albert Gosling nodded. 'Yes, I've already called the knacker. Can't really sell her to anyone else, not the way she looks now.'

'Exactly,' said Dolly. 'That's why I'm here. I'd like to take the mare to my place. You'd be rid of her right away, it wouldn't cost you a penny, and the horse would have a good life with me.'

28

Albert Gosling frowned. 'To be honest, I'm not bothered about that. If you want the nag then give me more than the knacker will pay. Simple.'

'Oh, simple, is it?' Dolly was still managing to look as if she thought Albert Gosling was a pleasant person. Emma could only admire her talent for play-acting. 'And how much would that be?'

Gosling shrugged his shoulders. He picked a spider off his suit and squashed it. 'The knacker will pay me three hundred pounds, so if you give me four hundred the mare is yours.'

'I tell you what.' Dolly pushed her white hair back from her forehead. 'I'll give you two hundred. I happen to have that on me.'

'What?' Gosling laughed. 'Is this supposed to be a bad joke? I don't have time for this.'

'Exactly,' said Dolly. 'You don't have time. Anyone can see that from looking at you. That's why I'm offering you two hundred pounds. The nearest knacker is Big Pete who lives a long, long way off, and he takes his time with everything. A lot of time. What did he tell you? That he'd come the day after tomorrow? Or the day after the day after tomorrow? Then you'd better add at least four days to that. You can never tell with Pete. Go on, call him.' Dolly pointed to the mobile that Gosling was taking out of his jacket pocket. 'Very nice phone you have there. Call Pete and ask him when he's coming to fetch Mississippi.'

Albert Gosling looked at Dolly, started tapping in a number, and then put it away again. 'Okay. Yeah, I heard the knacker man isn't a fast mover.' He straightened his tie. 'Give me two hundred and fifty.'

Emma held her breath and looked at her grandmother. Dolly seemed to be enjoying herself.

'Actually, I said two hundred. I ought to be the one around here who's hard of hearing, don't you think?'

Albert Gosling narrowed his eyes in annoyance. 'Daffy Dolly. You always were stubborn. My uncle once said your head was harder than the churchyard wall. Don't pick any quarrels with Dolly, he always used to say.'

'Yes, he knew me well,' said Dolly. 'In fact, very well. Wanted to take me to America with him once, but that's old history. Well, how about it? Two hundred?'

Gosling shrugged his shoulders again. 'Two hundred, then. I have better things to do than stand around haggling over peanuts with an old woman. Give me the money, but then you must take the old nag away with you, understand?'

'Oh, we'll do that,' Emma murmured. 'Happily.' Gosling didn't even look at her.

Dolly took her wallet out of her pocket and counted the banknotes out into his hand. 'And something else,' she said. 'I like to get these things in writing. I want a written receipt saying I have a legal right to the horse.'

Albert Gosling sighed. His mobile rang, but he ignored it. 'Anything else you fancy? Want me to gift-wrap the nag too, put a bow round her neck?'

'No, thank you,' said Dolly. 'That

won't be necessary. We'll take her as she is.'

Albert Gosling laughed nastily. 'What do you want the horse for, anyway?' he asked.

'Well, you see,' said Dolly, looking around Clipperbush's bedroom, 'I originally just wanted to save Mississippi from being slaughtered— which I'm sure is something you can't understand. But since she's cost me so much of my hard-earned money, I have another idea. My granddaughter here is crazy about horses, and my old gelding Aldo at home isn't good for much these days. So I'm going to give her the mare.'

Emma just stared at Dolly. She was speechless.

But Albert Gosling laughed again. 'Well, well,' he said with a sneer. 'Have fun, girly. She's not exactly anyone's dream pony.'

Emma ignored him. She was still standing there, speechless, thinking about what Dolly had just said.

'What do you want me to write?' asked Gosling. He turned his writing pad round.

Dolly dictated to him. 'I, Albert Gosling, hereby sell the mare Mississippi to Dolores Flowerdew for the price of two hundred pounds. Sign and date.'

When Gosling handed her the signed note, she read it through very carefully. Then she nodded, folded it up and put it in her trouser pocket.

'Thank you,' she said. 'And maybe you'll find treasure hidden in that mattress yet. Come along, Emma.'

They left the house as fast as they could. When Emma turned in the yard to look back, she saw Albert Gosling standing up at the window gazing down at them. 'I don't think he liked your joke about the mattress,' she told Dolly.

'So what? I didn't like him,' replied Dolly. 'Come on, we'll fetch Mississippi and go home. It's a long way on foot.'

The mare was standing in the last box of the empty stable. When Dolly and Emma came closer she pricked up her ears and stepped nervously from foot to foot. Dolly put out her hand

and let Mississippi nuzzle at it.

'Horses are a bit like dogs,' she said softly. 'They judge you from your smell. I hope she likes mine.'

'I think she looks pretty,' whispered Emma.

'Well, Mississippi,' said Dolly gently. 'How would you like to go for a walk?' She looked round. 'Emma, can you see a halter hanging up anywhere? And a lead rope wouldn't be a bad idea. Knapp was in such a hurry that I quite forgot to bring anything like that with me.'

Emma had to search for quite a long time before she finally found a halter and a rope with a snap hook on the end of it in one of the front boxes. Then, in a painted chest standing by the stable door, she also found something else: an old saddlebag, stuffed with coloured ribbons, little bells and fabric flowers, the smart saddle cloth that Clipperbush always used to put under Mississippi's saddle, a red bridle, and the saddle itself. It looked even more beautiful close to. Emma stroked the raised leather, admiring it.

34

'Found something?' asked Dolly.

'All sorts of things!' replied Emma. She took the halter, the rope and the saddlebag over to her grandmother. 'And there's still the saddle and bridle and lots of other things in that chest. But we didn't buy her tack as well, did we?'

'I think we did,' said Dolly. 'We'll put the saddle on Mississippi now, but leave the bridle in the saddlebag. We'll use the headcollar to lead her home.'

So Emma took everything she had found in Clipperbush's chest and put it down on the straw beside Mississippi's loose-box. 'I've never seen such a lovely saddle,' she said. 'But it's such a funny shape!'

Dolly nodded. 'That's a Western saddle—Clipperbush ordered it specially from America. The whole village roared with laughter the first time he rode about on that thing, but Clipperbush didn't mind. He was never interested in what people said. There, my beauty,' said Dolly, opening the door to the box and going in to Mississippi.

The mare stepped back and snorted, but when Dolly put the halter on her she kept still. Dolly carefully attached the rope, patted Mississippi's neck to reassure her, and then led her out of the box.

As she put the cloth and the saddle on the mare, Mississippi seemed a little nervous, but Dolly patted her and spoke softly to her, and she soon calmed down again.

'I can't ride her yet, can I?' asked Emma.

'No, darling.' Dolly shook her head, smiling. 'She has to get to know you properly first. And this is a very choosy lady when it comes to people who ride her. You'll have to be very sure she likes you before you attempt to get on her back.'

'Okay, never mind.' Emma slung the saddlebag around her and opened the stable door.

Mississippi breathed in the fresh air, snorting. She couldn't wait to get out into the open.

'Oh dear!' said Dolly. 'How long have you been standing around in this stable?'

When she led the mare across the yard, Mississippi looked round a few times, but she was quiet as a lamb as she followed Dolly through the gate.

'There we are!' said Dolly, relieved. They were following the narrow country road leading back to the village. 'Went like clockwork. But I'm going to need a brandy when I get home, to wipe out the memory of that Gosling idiot. Poor old Clipperbush, he really didn't deserve a nephew like that.' She turned to the mare. 'Pretty lady, isn't she? In spite of those zebra stripes. Did you know that a horse's hair always grows back white after an injury?'

Emma shook her head.

Dolly bent down to her. 'Is something wrong?'

Emma cleared her throat. 'Just now. I mean, what you said then. You were only saying it, weren't you?'

'What *did* I say?' Dolly smiled. 'I can't really remember.'

Emma went red. 'Well, that you were going to give me the horse.'

Dolly's smile grew even wider. 'Oh, did I say that? Well, if I said it, then I'm sure I meant it.'

Emma flung her arms around Dolly's neck—so hard that Dolly almost let go of the rope.

'Hold on, calm down!' she said. 'Or this horse will be charging off before you've even got to know her.'

Emma was so excited she could hardly breathe.

'Do you think,' she asked, when she had enough breath back, 'do you think Aldo and Mississippi will get on all right?' She put her hand into her jacket pocket. 'Oh, bother, I don't even have a carrot for her.'

She kept turning to look at the mare. Her mare. Mississippi pricked up her ears and looked right back at her.

'If they don't get on it won't be Aldo's fault,' said Dolly. 'We'll keep them apart for a few days. Just let them sniff at each other over the fence. After a while they'll work it out that two is more fun than being all alone.'

'Hey, Dolly.' Emma danced along in front of her grandmother. 'You must call Mr Knapp and give him his money back. You'll have to tell him we bought Mississippi.'

'I will, I will!' Dolly stopped as a car drove by, but Mississippi didn't shy at it. She was obviously used to cars. 'All the same—you'd better calm down a bit. It's not likely, but it could still be possible that Clipperbush didn't leave the horse to his nephew. In which case our sale agreement isn't valid. Have you thought of that?'

Emma looked at her in horror.

'No!' she murmured.

'Well, you ought to,' said Dolly. 'To be on the safe side. As I said, it's unlikely, because as far as I know Clipperbush had no other relations, but—don't get too excited just yet. Just for the time being, okay?'

Emma nodded.

She would certainly think about it. All the time. And not just a tiny little bit.

'Dolly?' she asked. 'Did old Clipperbush really want to take you to America with him?'

Her grandmother laughed. She

laughed so much that Mississippi
pricked up her ears. 'Yes, he did,' she
said. 'But I didn't want to go. Now,
forget it. It's so long ago that it isn't
even true any more.'

'All the same, I'd like to hear about it
sometime,' said Emma.

'Right, sometime,' said Dolly. 'But
for now you can lead this horse. My
arm is getting tired.'

Emma led Mississippi the rest of the
way home. She had butterflies in her
tummy, thousands of them, and her
mouth was dry with happiness, but she
still couldn't really believe it.

She suddenly had a horse.

A real horse. A horse of her own.

No. That sort of thing happens only
in books or films, she kept thinking.
Not in real life. And definitely not to
me. I can't even have a guinea pig.

But then she turned to look, and
there was Mississippi.

And Emma just looked at the mare,
and was happy—and tried not to think
how short the summer holidays could
be.

CHAPTER 4

'Oh, my goodness, how my feet hurt!' groaned Dolly as they reached the village pond. 'That was even worse than cycling. Knapp owes me at least three cat consultations for this.'

As she opened the door Shaggy rushed to meet her, barking.

'I'll have to train you not to make all that noise, fatso,' said Dolly. 'Or you'll be ending up in Lizzie's cookpot.'

Max and Leo were waiting on the bench under the walnut tree.

'Hi, Emma!' called Max. 'What are you doing with old Clipperbush's horse?'

'Ssh!' hissed Leo. He looked round in alarm. 'That's unlucky.'

'What's unlucky?' His big brother glanced at him in surprise.

'Saying a dead person's name.'

'Don't be daft!' Max grinned and rushed up to Emma. Mississippi pranced nervously.

Dolly soothed her by patting her

neck. 'Emma, I think you'd better take your horse to the paddock before you do anything else. Put her in the little one behind the goats' shed.'

'Okay.' Emma clicked her tongue and led Mississippi away. 'You two can come with me if you like,' she said, as she passed the boys. 'But stay quiet, right? Mississippi might get nervous.'

'You act as if we didn't know anything about horses,' Max called after her.

*   *   *

Aldo was standing under a tall lilac bush, dozing, when Emma opened the gate leading into the little paddock. Inquisitively, he raised his head and looked over the fence.

Emma tied Mississippi to the fence, took her saddle off, and then led her around her new pasture. The mare examined it uneasily.

'Well?' said Emma quietly. 'How do you like it here? It's still all a bit strange, I expect. The sounds, the smells . . .'

Mississippi pricked up her ears, took a couple of steps back and looked around. Then she widened her nostrils and snorted.

'And the grass here must taste different from your grass at home too,' said Emma. 'I know the feeling. About everything being strange, I mean. I bet I've moved house more often than you have.'

Now the mare had seen Aldo. She trotted a little way towards him, stopped and whinnied quietly. Aldo snorted and trotted up to the fence dividing the two paddocks.

'This is Aldo.' Emma walked slowly over the short grass behind Mississippi. 'He's older than you are and a bit lazy. But I'm sure you'll get on well together.'

The mare pricked up her ears again and looked at Emma as if she understood every word. Emma went up to her, stroked her soft mane and held her hand out under the snuffling nostrils. 'You don't know my name yet, do you? Are horses interested in names? Mine is Emma.'

Aldo stretched his neck across the fence and whinnied. Mississippi raised her head and turned. The two horses looked at each other.

'Hey, Emma!' called Max from outside the fence. 'What are you rabbiting on about? Horses don't like all that yak-yak-yak stuff.'

'Okay, okay!' Emma went back to the fence, climbed it and sat down beside Max. 'You don't know a thing about it. I don't even think you like horses.'

Max shrugged his shoulders. 'Not specially. Leo likes them.'

Leo leaned on the fence and looked at the two horses, who were now snuffling at each other over the fence between them.

'What did Dolly mean?' asked Max. 'I mean, saying that was your horse. My dad said Clipperbush's nephew is going to have her made into pet food.'

'He was going to,' said Emma, 'but Dolly bought Mississippi from him and gave her to me.'

'Well, good luck!' Max laughed. 'You'd better buy a dog lead for her.

She wouldn't let anyone but old Clipperbush ride her. Remember how she threw Harry off, Leo?'

'You bet.' Leo nodded without taking his eyes off the horses.

'Harry? Harry from the car repair shop?' asked Emma.

'That's right.' Max nodded. 'He was going round boasting he could ride like a cowboy. "Can you?" said old Clipperbush. "Then ride round the village pond on Mississippi." Harry ended up in the middle of the pond. He was all covered in mud when he got out again. Wow, was he furious.'

Emma shook her head and looked at Mississippi. The mare and Aldo were still snuffling at each other. Emma heard them both whinnying quietly.

'Did Mississippi ever throw Clipperbush's nephew off her back as well?' she asked.

Leo shook his head. 'He'd rather sit in a big car than on a horse. And he's been living in town for ever. He has some kind of business there; used to come and visit Clipperbush once a month. Then they always went to see

45

the grave of Clipperbush's sister together. Clipperbush rode Mississippi there and his nephew followed them by car.'

'Guess what I call him?' Max giggled. 'The Alligator. Because of his smile. You ought to see it some time. He smiles just like a crocodile. A real crocodile.'

Max imitated the smile, and Emma and Leo had to laugh.

'Looks like a genuine crocodile smile,' said Emma

They looked back at the horses. They were both grazing now on their separate sides of the fence.

'Good thing Aldo's a gelding,' said Leo. 'A gelding and a mare usually get on well together.'

Max grinned. 'Our dad says Clipperbush sometimes used to bring Mississippi into the house and give her a cup of coffee, can you imagine?'

Leo and Emma leaned over the fence, laughing.

'Why is she called Mississippi, anyway?' asked Emma.

'Because *Tom Sawyer* was

Clipperbush's favourite book,' said Leo.

'That's right, and that story happens beside the Mississippi River,' agreed Max. 'He told us that thousands of times. Bored us to death with it. Hey, listen.' He turned around. 'There's someone hooting his car horn like mad over there.'

*   *   *

Mr Knapp's car was standing outside Dolly's garden gate, with Tom and Jerry on the back seat.

'Dolly!' called the vet through the car window. 'Dolly, help!'

Lizzie Dockfoot peered over her garden gate inquisitively. 'What's all this noise about?' she asked. 'It's midday.'

'Hello, Lizzie!' called the vet, waving to her through the windscreen. 'Emma,' he said, lowering his voice, 'please could you be kind enough to fetch your grandmother?'

'Of course.' Emma went indoors and found Dolly.

'What is it?' she asked, coming out. 'Can't a person even spend ten minutes listening to the radio around here?'

'It's your dogs!' said Mr Knapp. 'I can't get your dogs out of the car. I've tried to put them out twice already, but they just won't budge! And the moment I leave them alone they're munching the head rests.'

'Oh yes, I know what they're like!' Dolly opened the back door of the car and whistled once, through her teeth. Tom and Jerry immediately jumped out of the car and bounded round Dolly, wagging their tails.

'Thank God!' Relieved, the vet leaned back. 'Well, tell me how you got on with Clipperbush's nephew. Did you get the mare?'

Dolly nodded.

'Hooray!' cried the vet, drumming his fingers on the steering wheel in delight. 'Then now we can do everything possible to make sure the old girl has a few good years still ahead of her, eh?'

'He wanted four hundred pounds,' said Emma. 'But Dolly beat him down to two hundred.'

'Great!' Mr Knapp grinned. 'Then I'll get a whole hundred back.'

'You'll get your three hundred back,' said Dolly, taking out her wallet. 'I decided to give the horse to Emma. Since I had to work so hard to save her, I thought the mare should stay in the family. And Aldo will be glad of her company.'

The vet looked at her in surprise.

'Well, you astonish me!' he said. 'I'll agree, but only on one condition.'

'And that is?' asked Dolly.

Emma looked at the vet, feeling worried.

'I take over all the expense of her feed for the next three months,' said Knapp. 'And Emma will brew me another of those wonderfully strong cups of coffee sometime soon. Agreed?'

Emma grinned. 'Agreed.'

'Shake hands on it!' Mr Knapp held his long, thin hand out to her through the window. 'Congratulations, you now own a horse. And between ourselves, Mississippi is a very good horse indeed.

Even though she may not look like it.'

'I think she looks very pretty,' said Emma.

'Well, excellent!' cried the vet. 'Old Clipperbush would jump over his grave for joy if he'd heard that. Oh, and by the way, he always used to give Mississippi a chocolate bar on Sundays. It would be a good idea to wean her off that.'

Then he waved to them out of the window again, put his foot down on the accelerator and drove away. A little faster than he usually drove.

CHAPTER 5

It wasn't until supper-time that Leo and Max finally went home. Their parents didn't see much of the two boys when Emma came to visit. Once they had left, Dolly and Emma fed the animals, Emma cooked her special scrambled eggs, and then they watched an old film on television. It had Hugh Grant in it, and a lot of love scenes.

Dolly cried over the happy ending, as usual, and then they went to bed.

Tom and Jerry were already lying on Emma's bed up in her room, breathing noisily, and the black cat had found a comfortable place to sleep on top of the wardrobe.

Emma loved her little attic room in Dolly's house—the flowered bedspread, the dusty bunches of lavender on the windowsill, the old photos of Emma's mother on the wall, the fat pillows. Her head nearly sank without trace in them. Usually she slept like a log up there, but tonight she couldn't sleep a wink.

She kept thinking of Mississippi the whole time. After all, you don't get a present of a horse every day. Emma would really have liked to make herself a bed in the straw next to Mississippi's box, but Dolly had said something about rats looking for food in the henhouse next door, and so she decided against that idea.

All the same, after a while, when it was still pitch dark outside, Emma couldn't stand it any longer. She put on

51

her dressing gown, got into her wellingtons and crept out of the house with a torch. Tom and Jerry sleepily followed her outside. As she crossed the yard, Emma looked up at the night sky. It was really black here at Dolly's house, not milky grey like the night sky in town, and it was covered with twinkling stars.

A couple of Dolly's cats came prowling out of the stables, looking for reckless mice. The door of the stable creaked as Emma opened it. She quietly slipped in. It smelled of fresh straw and horses.

One of them snorted in the dark. While Tom and Jerry rummaged around in the straw, Emma went over to Mississippi. Dolly had fitted out the last box for the mare, so that there was an empty one between her and Aldo. After all, they'd only known each other for a day.

Mississippi stood perfectly still, with her eyes closed, resting one leg. Her coat shone in the dark. Emma would have loved to pat her, but she didn't want to startle the mare, so she just looked.

'I tell you what,' she said quietly. 'I'm going to call you Missie. You don't mind, do you?'

The mare raised her head sleepily and opened her eyes. When she saw Emma, she flared her nostrils and pricked up her ears. Very cautiously, Emma put out her hand and stroked Mississippi's soft nose.

'What on earth do people think they're talking about? You're not beastly!' she said. 'Not a bit. You belong to me now, did you know that?'

The mare looked at Emma. Her ears twitched.

'I'm afraid I won't see you except in the holidays,' said Emma. 'But I'll send you carrots and sugar lumps every month. Do you like sugar lumps? Oh no—I'm sure they're not good for your teeth.'

Tom and Jerry nudged Emma with their noses.

'All right, all right, just coming,' she said.

When Mississippi caught the scent of the dogs it made her uneasy. She stepped back.

'You idiots.' Emma scratched Jerry behind the ears. 'Now you've scared her. Come on then, let's go back into the house. See you tomorrow, Missie,' she said. 'Sleep well.'

There was a rustling in the straw. It sounded a little scary, but Emma simply imagined a couple of cute little mice. She wasn't at all afraid of mice.

A crate now stood under the last window in the stable, containing Mississippi's saddle and bridle and the saddle-cloth. Dolly had brought it down from the attic. It wasn't as beautiful as the one Clipperbush had kept Mississippi's tack in, but Emma was going to paint it. She had already written Mississippi's name on it, in big curly letters. They were not particularly easy to read, admittedly, but they looked pretty. Emma opened the lid, pushed the bridle aside and stroked the saddle again.

Tom was scratching at the stable door and whining.

Emma closed the crate again with a sigh, opened the door for the dogs, and went back to the house with them.

It was dark in Dolly's room and in the kitchen. There was a light on in the hall, that was all. Sometimes, when Dolly couldn't sleep, she would sit at the kitchen table reading and drinking hot milk with honey. Today there was no one in the kitchen but Dolly's tabby cat, who was curled up on the sofa with her head on her tail. When Tom and Jerry looked through the doorway she hissed softly. Emma went past her, opened the fridge, drank a glass of milk and shooed the dogs upstairs.

The black cat was still lying on top of the wardrobe. Tom and Jerry jumped up on the bed as soon as Emma had wriggled under the covers again.

'Oh, Mississippi,' she murmured, snuggling down into her pillow—and she fell asleep so quickly that she didn't even have time to switch off the light.

CHAPTER 6

Next morning it was pouring with rain.

'Looks like the angels have pulled the plugs out of their bathtubs up there,' Dolly grumbled over breakfast. All the dogs were lying around, while the cats had made themselves comfortable up in the bedrooms. When Emma had gone out to the stables to feed the other animals, Jerry wouldn't even put his nose outside the door. However bad the weather, it didn't usually bother him.

'Did you take the horses out to the paddock?' asked Dolly.

Emma shook her head. 'In this weather? They'd catch a cold out there.'

Dolly laughed. 'No, darling, they don't mind the rain. But if they stand in the stable all day they'll get so bored that they'll start kicking the walls eventually.'

'Okay, then, I'll just go and turn them out.' Emma jumped up, slipped on her raincoat and wellingtons, and ran outside. The dogs just stared at her in surprise. They didn't even follow her to the front door.

Emma skipped through the puddles to the stable.

Three cats had found a spot in the empty box between Aldo and Mississippi.

Emma took first Aldo and then Mississippi out to the paddock. They really were both glad to get outside. The rain didn't seem to bother them at all. And Emma forgot it, too, when she watched the horses nuzzling at each other, scratching and rubbing their necks together over the fence between them. Only when water ran down her collar did she notice that she was sopping wet.

She ran back to the house. Outside the stable, she saw an unfamiliar cat sitting beside the muck heap. The cat followed Emma, mewing pitifully.

'Oh no, I don't think I've seen you before,' murmured Emma. 'That's going to mean one more can to open in the mornings, I bet!'

She ran a little faster, but the cat followed just as swiftly.

'Why do you all have to come to Dolly's house? Has word spread that this place is some kind of animal hotel?' Emma opened the front door, and the grubby little cat slipped past her into the dry.

'Dolly?' asked Emma, putting her jacket on the radiator. 'Do you have a little white cat?'

'Little white cat?' Dolly put her head out of the kitchen doorway. 'Do you mean that one? No, I've never seen it before.' She sighed. 'Oh dear, not another one! And scrawny as she is, she'll probably stay.'

The cat slipped into the kitchen, retreated when she saw the dogs and darted upstairs like lightning.

'And if I know my luck,' said Dolly, 'she's in kitten too. People just go off on holiday, leaving their animals, and I don't suppose this'll be the last one to find its way here.'

Looking thoughtful, she went back into the kitchen.

'Can I do anything to help you?'

asked Emma.

'Yes, please.' Dolly was just washing the cats' and dogs' dishes. 'You could peel some potatoes so that the animals aren't the only ones to eat around here.'

'No problem,' said Emma, and she set to work. Shaggy came along, sniffed the potato peelings, and lay down again under the kitchen table, disappointed.

'Knapp called just now,' said Dolly. 'About another man who wants to get rid of his dog. I'm afraid I'll soon have to put up a notice saying "Closed Because of Overcrowding". Two of the cats are in kitten, Tom needs tablets for his heart trouble, Shaggy has to have his inoculation booster. And Mississippi . . .' Here Dolly stopped short. 'Oh, why am I going on about all that again? How about a hot cocoa to keep the cold weather out?'

She let the water in the sink run away and dried her hands.

Emma looked at her, worried. When Dolly saw her face she laughed. 'Dear, dear, you don't want to take any notice of my moaning. Rainy weather always puts me in a bad temper, and what I say then is just nonsense. Ask Knapp. He'll tell you so!'

'It's not nonsense at all,' said Emma. 'I tell you what, I'll send you my pocket money. You can use it to buy feed for Mississippi. Or some of her feed, anyway, okay?'

But Dolly just shook her head and ran her fingers through her hair. 'Never mind that!' she said. 'I'll manage. But I ought to think over Knapp's offer again.'

'What offer?' asked Emma suspiciously. People had often given Dolly good advice about how to get rid of her never-ending worries about money. Lizzie Dockfoot had suggested that she could sell the horses' paddocks behind the stable as a building site for six semi-detached houses. Mr Procter, who owned the car repair shop next door, wanted to buy some of Dolly's land for a car wash, and Leo and Max's father thought Dolly ought to breed poodles.

'Well,' said Dolly, drying the animals' bowls and lining them up by the kitchen door again. 'Knapp suggested that as well as my regular guests here, I might run a kind of boarding house for animals when their owners go away. Charging the owners a fee. A pound a day for a guinea pig, four pounds for cats, five pounds for dogs—something like that, if you see what I mean.'

'But that's a very good idea!' cried Emma.

'Do you think so?' Dolly shrugged her shoulders. 'Well, I don't know. That kind of thing can easily get too much for a person. People would be saying, "My dog only eats this," and "My cat has to be brushed every morning." And at the moment I have three male dogs about the place. What happens if a bitch in season suddenly turns up here, and all the dogs are after her? I don't think people would be too pleased for their pets to be presenting them with puppies or kittens all of a sudden, two months after they get back from holiday.'

'Yes, I see,' murmured Emma.

'I tell you what.' Dolly sat down with Emma at the table and tickled Shaggy behind the ears. 'It's about time you painted me some of your lovely rehoming ads again. You know: "Pretty kitten seeks caring new owners", or "Who could resist a cute little shaggy-haired puppy?"'

'Of course!' Emma nodded. 'I'd love to.'

She wrote stacks of advertisements like that for Dolly every summer, hung them up on trees or put them in the window of the bakery, and in the other shops and even the church porch.

'And this time you must do me a few of them in black and white,' said Dolly. 'Procter in the car repair shop has bought himself a photocopier for his desk. If you go over with a few fresh eggs and tell him what a marvellous machine you think it is, I'm sure he'll let you print out a few copies. And then I'll put them through people's letter boxes along with their newspapers. The way things are going at the moment, there are going to be a lot of kittens here this summer, and the odd holiday-stray is sure to land up here as well.'

'Rely on me,' said Emma. 'I'll get

down to work straight away.'

And so she did.

But first she went to see Mississippi again.

CHAPTER 7

Directly after lunch, Emma went over to Mr Procter's car repair shop. It was still raining buckets, and Emma pulled the hood of her raincoat well down over her forehead.

There were oily puddles in the parking place outside the workshop. Emma hurried past the cars and tractors standing there—and ran straight into someone.

'Can't you look where you're going?'

Emma raised her head, and found herself looking into the Alligator's face. There he stood, dressed to the nines, with gold cufflinks, a big watch on his wrist and a suit as black as a gravedigger's. Rainwater was running off his umbrella and dripping down on Emma.

'Sorry!' she muttered.

'Oh, it's you, is it?' said Albert Gosling, smiling his crocodile smile. 'Daffy Dolly's granddaughter. Well, what a granny you have—giving you such an ugly old nag! But maybe you can paint out the zebra stripes, what do you think?'

Emma just looked darkly at him.

The Alligator leaned back against his big car. Harry, Mr Procter's apprentice, was standing beside him, stroking its silver-grey paint reverently. Emma knew Harry because he sometimes brought spare parts over for Dolly's car.

'Excuse me, can I get past, please?' She forced her way between the two men and made for the car repair shop. When she looked back, she saw Harry still worshipping the silly car.

Emma stuck her tongue out at the Alligator—although unfortunately he didn't see her—and went into the dark workshop.

'Mr Procter!' she called. She looked enquiringly round in the dark. A telephone rang somewhere.

Emma found a little office behind the hydraulic lift. She knocked on the greasy door.

'Lunch break!' someone called. 'Come back in an hour's time.'

Plucking up her courage, Emma cautiously put her head round the door. 'It's me, Mr Procter,' she said. 'Emma, Dolly's granddaughter. I've come about the photocopier.'

'Oh, hello, Emma!' Mr Procter swung his short legs off his desk and put the rest of his sandwich into his mouth. 'Come along in! My word, you must have grown at least twelve inches since last time! If I don't watch out you'll be spitting down on my bald head any day now.'

Emma grinned and put a box of eggs down on the desk. 'Dolly said I was to give you these and ask if I can copy something?'

'Of course!' Mr Procter took Emma over to a little table by the window. 'Here we are—my pride and joy!' He lovingly flicked a duster over the copier. 'Great, don't you think? Do you know how these things work?'

Emma nodded. 'We have a copier just like that at school.'

'Good, fire away, then. What do you want to copy?'

'Oh, only a couple of notices—about Dolly's cats, you see. And a few of my grandmother's other papers. She's always losing things, so she wanted me to copy them.'

Mr Procter grinned. 'Yes, she was never the tidiest of women. But a real live wire, no girl in the village to equal her. It's a real shame she never wanted to marry again.'

Emma looked at the stout little man in surprise.

He ran his hand over his bald head, looking embarrassed. 'Well, yes, I proposed to her myself once. And I wasn't the only one. Old Clipperbush, for instance, he tried his luck twice, but,' he added, switching the copier on, 'why am I telling you all this old history? How boring for a young girl like you, eh?'

'I don't think it's boring at all,' said Emma. 'I like listening to old history. Dolly never tells me anything like that.'

66

'Well then, I won't go on about it either,' said Mr Procter. 'You do your copying, and I'll just go and see what Harry's up to. It's suspiciously quiet out there.'

Emma watched him thoughtfully as he went out.

'Harry!' she heard him shout. 'Stop standing about patting other people's cars. We've got work piling up to the rafters in here!'

Emma grinned and set to work. When she had finished her copying, she took another, carefully folded piece of paper out of her pocket. It was the sale agreement for Mississippi. Dolly had put it up on her pin-board in the kitchen, but Emma wanted a copy as well, to take home. She was going to put it over her bed, just in case she woke up one day and thought that having her own horse had been only a dream. She was sure that would happen hundreds of times.

In the new, strange flat on the fourth floor, far away from Dolly and Mississippi.

CHAPTER 8

There were two dripping wet umbrellas in the hall, and loud voices came from the living room. That sounded like Alma and Henrietta, Dolly's best friends.

What are they doing here? Emma wondered. It's only Tuesday. Usually the two of them came to see Dolly and play cards on a Thursday. Emma stole up to the door and listened, but she couldn't make out what they were saying, because Dolly had put an opera CD on the hi-fi.

The new white cat came out of the kitchen, rubbed around Emma's legs and mewed. Emma picked her up and went into the living room.

Alma and Henrietta were sitting side by side on the sofa, and Dolly was just pouring them a glass of sherry each.

'Well, who have we here?' cried Henrietta. 'Let's have a look at you, Emma love. You're looking good. As delicious as a little cream slice.'

'But rather pale, don't you think?' said Alma.

'Nonsense, Alma,' boomed Henrietta. 'Not everyone is pink as a pig, like you.'

Offended, Alma pursed her lips.

'Take no notice of those two,' said Dolly. 'They're bored, that's all. That's why they're here. Did Procter let you make the copies?'

Emma nodded. 'Do you know what he said to me? He said you were a real live wire and there was no one in the village to equal you.'

'Did he, indeed?' Dolly shook her head. 'Then I'm not buying so much as a screwdriver from him any more.'

'And guess who else was there?' Emma tickled the white cat under the chin.

'Well, who?' Dolly poured herself a brandy, pushed Tom and Jerry out of her armchair, and sat down.

'The Alligator,' said Emma.

'Good heavens above!' Alma's eyes opened wide. 'Who on earth do you mean?'

'Clipperbush's nephew,' said Emma.

'That's what Max and Leo call him.'

'And a very good name for him too,' muttered Dolly. 'What was he doing at Procter's place? Had his fine car broken down?'

Emma shrugged her shoulders. 'No idea. He was just standing around letting Harry admire him.'

Dolly shook her head thoughtfully. 'I thought he'd have gone back to town ages ago.'

'Oh no!' fluted Alma. She leaned forward, lowering her voice. 'They say he's turning his uncle's house upside down looking for something. And he won't go back to town until he's found it.'

'What a fool.' Dolly took a large gulp of cognac. 'Clipperbush would never have hidden his money in the house. He wouldn't have been paid any interest if he had, and he liked to earn interest. He was as happy as a sandboy when he made a good profit.'

'What do you think, Dolly?' Stout Henrietta looked mysterious. 'Will he inherit the farm?'

'Oh, so that's why you two are here!'

cried Dolly. 'You think I know something about Clipperbush's will. Sorry, I can't contribute anything to the village gossip on that subject.'

'Are you sure?' Alma leaned back again.

'What a shame!' sighed Henrietta. 'We thought—'

'I know what you thought,' Dolly interrupted her. 'But I can only tell you that Clipperbush was fonder of his nephew than he deserved. And I should think he'll have left him everything because, after all, he's his favourite sister's son.'

Alma and Henrietta looked at each other. 'But Clipperbush's housekeeper was dropping such odd hints all over the place,' said Alma. 'She said there was a snag in the will, some kind of condition—Clipperbush had put it in on purpose, and he had a lot of fun thinking it up.'

'*What* kind of condition?' asked Emma, worried. The white cat jumped off her lap and went over to look at the budgie cage.

Dolly shooed the cat away. 'Oh, just

gossip. See what you do with all your talk? You'll send this poor child crazy.'

'How do you mean?' Henrietta and Alma looked at Emma in surprise.

'I mean I bought Clipperbush's old mare. For her. Dammit!' Dolly poured herself a coffee. 'Gosling was going to let the knacker have her. But if I know you two, you've heard all about that already.'

Henrietta said nothing, but Alma's eyes widened in surprise. 'No!' she cried. 'You bought that horse!'

'Yes, I did.' Dolly nodded. 'Your sources of gossip aren't up to much if you haven't heard about that already, Alma.'

'Oh, they never hear about anything in her retirement home.' Henrietta adjusted the ribbon bow over her mighty bosom. 'I have to keep her up to date with all the latest news.'

Henrietta had opened a little farm shop on her son-in-law's farm, and the whole village bought things from her. She always knew everything that was going on.

'Good heavens, two horses, Dolly!'

72

Alma sighed. 'Aren't you overdoing things a bit these days?'

'The horse belongs to Emma,' said Dolly. 'What's more, it's nothing to do with you, Alma. I don't go nattering on about the garden gnomes on your balcony.'

The white cat jumped up on the arm of Dolly's chair, stared at the table and licked her little muzzle.

'Drink up your sherry, you two,' said Dolly. 'And then I'm throwing you out. I have better things to do than gossip about housekeepers.'

Alma and Henrietta obediently reached to drain their glasses. At the same moment the white cat leaped up and landed among the coffee cups.

Alma let out a shrill scream.

'Get that cat off the table, Dolly!' she screeched. 'Get her off it!'

Emma had to put her hands over her mouth to keep from laughing.

'Well, don't go having a heart attack, Alma,' said Dolly. 'She's new here, poor little thing, she doesn't know the rules yet. Come along, little one, off you go. That milk jug wasn't meant for you.'

Stout Henrietta spluttered with laughter, so much that she almost choked.

'I'll say this for you, Dolly!' she gasped. 'There's always something going on in your house.'

'Exactly,' said Dolly. 'So calm down, Alma, all right? Nothing has happened.'

'Oh, all these animals really and truly send me mad!' groaned Alma. 'Oh—a budgie just landed in my hair!'

'Don't worry, it's gone again,' said Dolly. 'The birds have to fly now and then, after all.'

Alma frantically patted her hair back into place. Emma got up and looked out of the window. 'Can I go and see how the horses are doing?' she asked. 'And after that I'll put the notices up in the baker's and the church.'

Dolly nodded. 'And give Henrietta some of them to take away with her. The whole village meets in her shop.'

'You're never going to let the child go out in this weather?' Alma looked at Emma, horrified. 'Do you want her to catch her death?'

'Alma, she's not made of sugar!' sighed Dolly.

But by that time Emma was already out of the house.

CHAPTER 9

Five days later, the Alligator turned up.

Dolly and Emma had just gone out to the big paddock to put fresh water in the trough, an old bathtub that Dolly had cleared out of the house years ago. Mississippi and Aldo were standing side by side in a friendly way, watching. They had been in the same paddock for three days now, and they were getting on very well indeed.

Not even Shaggy barked when Albert Gosling opened Dolly's gate. The Alligator just scattered a handful of dog biscuits in the yard, and he had three new friends wagging their tails as they followed him across Dolly's property.

So Emma and Dolly didn't notice

the new arrival until he leaned over the fence of the paddock.

'Hello, Mrs Flowerdew,' he said.

Emma was so startled that she almost dropped her bucket when she saw him. This visit boded no good.

Dolly was probably thinking the same. She looked suspiciously at her unexpected guest.

'Well, what a surprise,' she said, and wiped her wet hands on her trouser legs. 'What brings you here? I thought you wanted to get back to town in a hurry.'

'And so I did,' agreed Albert Gosling. 'But there were still a few things to be settled here. My uncle left a good deal of disorder behind him. And my car is giving trouble. I had to take it to Procter a few days ago, and he hasn't got the spare part yet. After all, it's not a model of car you'd see very often in these parts.' There was his crocodile smile again. He pushed Shaggy's nose aside and looked round the place. 'Nice property you have here. You could really make something of it.'

Mississippi and Aldo were standing at the edge of the wood, grazing. Between them stood the goats, craning their necks to eat the leaves off the branches.

'I *have* made something of it, as you can see,' said Dolly. 'Well, could you get back to the subject, please? What brings you here?'

Gosling shooed a fly away from his suit and inspected his cufflinks with interest. 'It will seem strange to you, but I'm here to buy Mississippi back again.'

Emma's heart began to beat frantically like a little wild animal inside her.

'Oh, really?' said Dolly. 'What for?'

'Well, you see,' said Albert Gosling, propping a well-polished shoe on the paddock fence. 'I made a really stupid mistake. I mean, I simply owe it to my late uncle to look after the mare. He was so fond of Mississippi. I'm sure he wouldn't like to see her end up in the hands of strangers.'

For a moment Dolly said nothing at all. She just looked at Gosling with

77

only a hint of a smile on her lips. 'As you can see, Mississippi is fine,' she said at last. 'You're welcome to convince yourself of it. I think that's what would have been the most important thing to your uncle.'

'Oh, I don't doubt that you treat her well. But that's not the point.' The Alligator inspected the toes of his shoes as if there was something of interest to be seen there.

'What is the point, then?' asked Dolly. 'You surely don't seriously expect me to believe that your conscience is pricking you. Clipperbush wasn't even sure whether you had such a thing.'

Gosling went on looking at his shoes. When he did raise his head, he smirked. 'Ah, yes, I see. You want to haggle. I'd do the same myself.' He looked at his watch. 'I'll offer you three hundred pounds. A good bargain for you, right?'

Emma looked anxiously at Dolly. But Dolly just laughed out loud. Very loud.

'Yes, it certainly would be,' she said.

'But I can't sell the horse back to you.' She put her arm round Emma's shoulders. 'Because she belongs to my granddaughter. If you want to have Mississippi back, you'll have to do a deal with her.'

The Alligator narrowed his eyes.

Then he cleared his throat. When he spoke again, his voice sounded rather impatient. 'Very well. Your name is Emma, isn't it?'

Emma gave him a hostile look.

'Emma, will you sell me the horse? I'll give you four hundred pounds. That's a whole lot of money for a little girl.'

Emma shrugged her shoulders. 'I don't care. I'm not selling Mississippi.'

'That's silly, that's totally silly!' Albert Gosling ran his tongue over his teeth and looked across the paddock at Mississippi.

When he looked at Emma again, he had fixed his crocodile smile on his lips. But a rather pale version of it.

'Think it over,' he said. 'You don't look stupid. For that money, you can buy yourself another horse, a much better one! One to show off to your friends. I mean, just look at that mare!'

'I think she's pretty,' said Emma.

Someone snorted behind her. Mississippi pushed her head inquisitively over Emma's shoulder and nibbled her sweater. Emma lovingly patted her nose.

'You see? I like her and she likes me. And she's not a bit bad-tempered. Just a little quirky sometimes, and she does like to nibble sweaters. But apart from that . . .'

Now Aldo joined them. He was coming up to the fence.

Albert Gosling took his foot off the bottom rung of the fence and hurriedly stepped back.

'But she's my horse!' he shouted. 'And I want her back.'

'Why?' Emma shouted back. So loud that Mississippi threw her head up in alarm. 'You don't even like her!'

The Alligator had no answer to that. He turned, strode a few paces in such a rage that he almost fell over his fine shoes—and came back again.

'It's my last offer,' he said. 'Five

80

hundred pounds.' He looked at Dolly. 'Tell your pig-headed granddaughter what a lot of money that is.'

But Dolly just shook her head. 'I'm not getting mixed up in this. It's Emma's business.'

Albert Gosling looked at Emma. It was the meanest look anyone had ever given her, and it sent a cold shiver down her spine.

'Well, how about it?'

Emma looked back at him, in turn, as darkly as she possibly could.

'I'll never sell you Missie,' she said. 'Not even for a hundred million pounds. You can talk till you're blue in the face, and I still won't!'

The Alligator stared at her for a moment longer. Then he turned without a word, kicked one of the empty buckets standing on the grass and marched away.

'We'll talk about this some other time!' he shouted before getting into his car.

He drove away, revving his engine.

'Come along,' Dolly told Emma. 'Time we finished our work.'

They tipped a few more bucketfuls of fresh water into the horse-trough, gave Aldo and Mississippi a little garlic to nibble to make the flies leave them alone and then, in silence, they set off back to the house.

'Emma,' said Dolly, sighing. 'This whole thing smells of trouble. Gosling's guilty conscience never drove him here, that's for sure. Maybe it really is something to do with Clipperbush's will. I only wish I knew what!'

Emma looked at her grandmother, worried. 'But I couldn't let that man have Mississippi back.'

'Of course you couldn't!' said Dolly. 'Mississippi belongs to you, and that's that. No, you did the right thing. But there's going to be trouble, I'll bet my life on it. Do you know what? I'm going to make myself a coffee, and a cocoa for you, and then we'll sit under the walnut tree for a while and think this business over. All right?'

*　　　*　　　*

They hadn't been sitting at the table

for a minute before Lizzie Dockfoot leaned over the gate. 'What was Clipperbush's nephew here for?'

Dolly sighed.

'Go away, Lizzie, I don't need this,' she said. 'Don't you have to sweep your garden path?'

'Come on, tell me.' Lizzie Dockfoot picked up a rotting apple core with her fingertips and put it in Dolly's dustbin. 'What was he after?'

Dolly sighed. It was useless. Nothing could ever be kept secret from Lizzie Dockfoot anyway. 'He wanted to buy the horse back,' she said. 'That's what he was after. Happy now?'

'Wanted to buy the horse back?' Lizzie looked first at Dolly and then at Emma in surprise. 'Whatever for? He couldn't stand the mare.'

'Yes, we're asking ourselves the same question,' said Dolly. 'Whatever for? But we haven't thought of any answer yet. Do you have any idea?'

'He wanted to hand her over to the knacker,' said Lizzie. 'Maybe he still does. She once gave him a nasty nip. I know that for sure, because

Clipperbush told me so himself. When he wasn't dead yet, of course.'

Dolly shook her head. 'Would that be worth five hundred pounds to him?'

'Five hundred pounds? Good heavens above!' Lizzie Dockfoot turned pale. 'He offered you five hundred pounds? Why, your whole menagerie isn't worth that much.'

'Exactly.' Dolly rubbed her forehead thoughtfully. 'I just can't figure it out,' she murmured. 'Come on, Emma, let's get ourselves something to eat.'

'Oh, and before I forget, Dolly,' Lizzie called after them, 'those mongrels of yours were digging up my rose beds again yesterday. If I catch that precious pair at it again I'm going to make mincemeat out of them.'

'Why? You ought to be glad!' Dolly called back over her shoulder. 'It means you don't have to dig the beds over yourself, Lizzie.'

Whatever Lizzie's answer, Emma and Dolly didn't hear it. They had already closed the front door behind them.

CHAPTER 10

'What would you like to eat today?' asked Emma next morning at breakfast. When she was visiting Dolly she did the cooking almost every day. She could cook much, much better than her grandmother.

'Oh, for heaven's sake, what a dreadful question!' sighed Dolly. 'You know I can never make my mind up. Just give me a surprise, okay?'

'Okay,' said Emma. 'I think I already know what to cook. Are we going shopping today?'

Dolly nodded. 'We've run out of cat food again, I have to order feed for the horses, and we need coffee as well. Urgently!'

'And I'd like to buy a roll of film,' said Emma. 'So that I can take photos of Mississippi. You do have an old camera, don't you?'

Dolly shrugged her shoulders. 'Yes. I don't know just where it is, but I have one somewhere. Hey, Tom and Jerry,' she said, looking under the table where the dogs were waiting eagerly for any leftovers from breakfast. 'We're going to take Shaggy with us today, all right? To give my rug a bit of a rest. You two could make yourselves useful while we're out. Look for that camera, will you?'

*　　　*　　　*

They had been out almost all morning. When they had finally bought everything they needed, Dolly's estate car was almost full and her wallet was almost empty.

'My goodness!' she sighed as they set off for home. 'Do prices have to go up every day? If this goes on I'll have to feed the cats on grass and the dogs on leaves.'

Dolly drove along the main road so fast that Emma held on to her seat. Mum said Dolly's driving was hair-raising. Dolly said it was 'sporty'. But today she was definitely overdoing the sporty bit.

'Could you maybe drive a little

slower?' asked Emma. 'I'd quite like to get the chance to grow older.'

'Oh, sorry!' Dolly took her foot off the accelerator. 'I've just remembered that Knapp must have been sitting outside our front door for the last fifteen minutes. He promised to come and give the dogs their booster inoculations today. My word, he's going to be cross! I need to think up a good excuse.'

Dolly couldn't think up a good excuse. Nor could Emma. However, when they finally drove into the yard there was no sign of the vet, or his car either.

'Oh no!' groaned Dolly. 'He's gone again. What a mess!'

Between them they carried crates full of food and animal feed to the front door. But when Dolly went to unlock it, the door opened of its own accord. 'Am I going senile?' she muttered. 'I did lock the door, didn't I?'

'I think so,' said Emma. 'You always lock the door,' she pointed out, 'because otherwise Jerry can open it.'

Dolly shook her head, picked up a crate—and put it down again. Shaggy looked enquiringly up at her.

'Did you hear that?' she whispered.

'Hear what?' Emma looked past Dolly and down the corridor in alarm. But she couldn't hear anything suspicious. However, the kitchen door stood ajar.

'The coffee machine!' whispered Dolly. 'It's on!'

Dolly's coffee machine made a terrible racket. Nothing else in the house made a noise like that.

'So maybe I forgot to lock the front door,' muttered Dolly. 'But the dogs won't have been making themselves coffee, will they?'

Emma shook her head.

'You wait here.' Dolly stepped firmly through the doorway. 'Come on, Shaggy.'

Rather scared, Emma held her back by her jacket.

'Are you crazy?' she whispered. 'You can't go in there now. I'm going to run round to Procter's and call the police from there.'

'Oh, come on. Shaggy and I will be all right,' said Dolly. 'You stay here.'

She stole over to the coat stand, felt around on the shelf where she left hats and triumphantly held up her spray canister of mace spray.

Emma's heart almost stopped beating.

The coffee machine was still gurgling away.

Dolly took her spray canister in her right hand, and went towards the open kitchen door. Shaggy was waiting beside it, wagging his tail. This was more than Emma could stand. She was right behind her grandmother in a flash.

Dolly suddenly flung the kitchen door open. 'Don't move!' she cried. 'Or you get a load of mace spray right in your face.'

'Dolly!' said Mr Knapp, jumping up from the chair where he was sitting. 'What on earth's got into you?'

Shaggy disappeared under the kitchen table.

Astonished, Dolly and Emma stared at the vet.

'How did you get in here?' asked Dolly, once she had recovered the power of speech.

'What a question!' Knapp sank back into his chair with a sigh. 'Through the door.'

'But what about your car?' Dolly was still holding her canister of mace spray. 'You never come here without your car.'

'It's back with Procter,' growled Mr Knapp. 'The wretched thing keeps breaking down. So I left it over at the workshop and walked round here to inoculate your dogs. I was rather surprised to find you weren't in, but when I found out that the door wasn't locked I walked in and gave Tom and Jerry their jabs. Which wasn't easy, I can tell you. After that I thought I'd reward myself with a coffee and wait for you two to come back.' He looked under the table. 'It's no good hiding, Shaggy. Your turn in a moment.'

'The door was unlocked?' Dolly looked round the kitchen.

'Of course!' said Knapp.

90

'But I didn't leave it like that,' said Dolly. She opened the door of the kitchen cupboard, looked in, and closed it again.

'What?' Knapp looked at her, at a loss. 'What's that supposed to mean?'

Dolly took the full jug of coffee out of the coffee machine, took two mugs off the shelf and sat down at the table with Knapp. Emma was still standing in the doorway.

'I forgot about you,' Dolly told the vet. 'Sorry. I drove like mad all the way back hoping I might just be in time to catch you. But I did lock the door. I'm absolutely sure of that.'

'Oh, good Lord.' Knapp looked at her disbelievingly. 'Burglars, you mean? Breaking in here? But what is there to steal from you? Cats in kitten and old chickens?'

Dolly shrugged her shoulders.

'You know I'm not the tidiest of people, Knapp, but I can see that someone's been searching the cupboards and drawers here. He didn't even close the big chest of drawers in the hall properly. And I don't imagine

91

that was your doing.'

Speechless, the vet stared at his coffee.

'Good heavens above,' he murmured. 'That means I could have run straight into the man!' He swallowed.

'Oh, the dogs would have defended you,' said Dolly.

'*Your* dogs?' Knapp made a face. 'That precious pair didn't even bark when I came in. They just looked at me in a bored sort of way from the living-room door. And when they saw who it was they hid under the table. I had to haul the two of them out. One after another, because they're afraid of a little injection. And after that they hid again in a hurry. You think they're capable of defending anyone?'

'Well, I suppose they're not the best watchdogs in the world.'

Emma went to the kitchen window and looked out at the paddock. Mississippi and Aldo were grazing peacefully under the trees, side by side. Reassured, she turned round again.

'Has anything been stolen?' she

asked.

Dolly shrugged her shoulders again. 'I don't know yet. I'd taken my cash with me. And there's not much else worth anything here. But I'll look around later. Knapp, since we happen to be here together,' she added, stirring her coffee, 'do you know anything about Clipperbush's will?'

'Me? No, why?' The vet looked at her in surprise.

'Oh, well, Henrietta and Alma were here a few days ago, dropping mysterious hints,' said Dolly. 'They said Clipperbush's housekeeper had been saying there was a snag of some kind in the will. I didn't think much of it, but then his nephew suddenly turns up here yesterday wanting to buy Mississippi back.'

'What?' The vet was so surprised that he almost tipped over his chair.

'Yes, and when I said no he turned really nasty,' said Emma.

'Hm.' Mr Knapp tugged at one earlobe. 'That really is odd. I'll keep my ear close to the ground. Clipperbush's housekeeper is always bringing her dog round to me, although the animal is perfectly healthy. Perhaps she'll tell me what she knows. Well,' he said, draining his mug of coffee and standing up, 'I'll be right back. But first I'll take a look at Mississippi, all right, Emma?'

Emma jumped up at once. 'Yes, of course,' she said. 'I'll come with you.'

*　　　*　　　*

Mr Knapp was very pleased with Mississippi.

'Your horse looks at least five years younger since she came here,' he told Emma. 'Putting some kind of miracle-working stuff in her fodder, are you?'

Emma shook her head, embarrassed. 'I do give her a bit of garlic now and then to keep the flies away. And she gets plenty of carrots, and I walk her out every evening.'

'Excellent.' The vet patted the mare's neck. Mississippi turned her head and tried to nibble his pockets, looking for treats. 'Aha!' Mr Knapp took a step back, smiling. 'You're still trying that trick, are you? How long does she spend in the stable?'

'Oh,' said Emma, shrugging her shoulders, 'she's turned out all the time. I usually bring her in at night, specially since Clipperbush's nephew came here. But the horses are both out in the paddock again first thing in the morning. Even if it's raining. Dolly says that does them good.'

'Dolly is right.' Knapp nodded. 'Most horses spend far too long in the stable. Old Clipperbush sometimes didn't take Mississippi out of her box except when he wanted to ride her, or invite her into the house to keep him company over his coffee. I was always telling him she needed fresh air, grass and the company of other horses, but he wouldn't hear of it. "Fresh air will make her catch a cold," he'd grumble, "and my company is quite enough for her." He loved that mare, but he didn't know anything about horses. And he was terribly pig-headed.'

Emma looked out at the paddock, where Aldo and Mississippi were grazing in perfect harmony.

95

'What if I can't keep her?' she said quietly.

'Oh, come on!' Mr Knapp put his long arm round her shoulders. 'Of course you can keep her. All this talk about the will is nothing but village gossip. There's not too much that goes on here for people to talk about. So they invent things now and then to make life interesting. Don't you worry about it. All right?'

Emma nodded.

'I hear you and your parents are moving house. Will it be further for you to come here?'

'No.' Emma shook her head. 'In fact I'll be a little closer.'

'That's great,' said Mr Knapp. 'Maybe you can even come here at weekends.'

'I certainly will,' said Emma. She immediately felt a bit better.

CHAPTER 11

'Burglars?' said Max. 'Wow, how exciting. What a shame nothing like that ever happens at our house.'

'So what was stolen?' asked Leo.

'Nothing,' said Emma. 'That's the funny part of it.'

The afternoon sun was high in the sky, and the three of them were sitting beside the village pond, throwing stones into the muddy water.

'I bet the Alligator is behind this,' said Max. 'He's mad because you won't give him the horse back. Maybe it was some kind of revenge.'

'That's just silly!' Leo shook his head. 'Then he'd have smashed the whole place up, wouldn't he? No, Dolly forgot to lock the door, that's all. Her cupboards and drawers always look as if someone's been rummaging around in them.'

'But the dog biscuits!' Emma pointed out. 'There was an empty bag in the dustbin, and Dolly never buys that brand.'

'Well, there you are, Mister Cleverclogs, that proves it!' Max tapped his brother on the nose. 'Everyone in this village knows that Dolly's dogs won't kick up any fuss so long as you give them something to eat.'

But Leo shook his head. 'I'm sure the Alligator doesn't know that. Anyway, what would he have been after in Dolly's house?'

Neither of the other two knew the answer to that.

'Why do you have to be so logical?' muttered Max. 'Enough to drive anyone round the bend. Didn't old Lizzie see anything? Usually she's always poking her nose over the fence.'

'No.' Emma sighed. 'She'd gone to visit her sister.' She pulled up a dandelion leaf and nibbled it thoughtfully. She did that for quite some time. Then she suddenly stood up and brushed bits of grass off her trousers. 'I'm going to ride over there,' she said. 'On Aldo.'

The boys looked at her in surprise.

'Ride over where?' asked Max.

'To Clipperbush's house,' said Emma. 'I'm sure the Alligator is planning something. He's frantic to have Mississippi back. No idea why, but I bet he has something to do with our weird burglary. And I'm going to find out what this is all about. And that's why I am riding over there now!' She turned and hurried back to Dolly's house, with the boys running after her.

'Hey, wait for us!' called Max.

But Emma didn't wait. She climbed over the gate, ran past the house and fetched Aldo's bridle from the stable. She didn't need a saddle; Dolly had taught her to ride the gelding bareback.

When Emma opened the gate to the paddock, Mississippi and Aldo raised their heads, surprised. The goats came picking their way up to Emma, bleating, until the ropes tethering them were fully stretched.

'No, sorry, I don't have anything for you today,' said Emma as she went on past them.

'What are you going to say to him?' Max called to her over the fence.

' "Hey, Mister Alligator, have you been burgling my grandmother's house?" '

Emma didn't reply. Aldo and Mississippi trotted inquisitively towards her. Emma gently pushed Missie's snuffling nose aside and tried to get Aldo's bridle on him. First Aldo put his head up when she tried to get the bit into his mouth, but then he seemed to remember that this uncomfortable thing meant he was going for a ride, and stood there like a lamb as she put the bridle over his head. Mississippi watched with interest.

'Aldo will soon be back, Missie,' said Emma. 'He just has to take me somewhere for a little while. One of these days you and I will go for a ride together too, all right? If you feel like it.'

As she led Aldo out of the field, the mare followed them to the gate.

'Hold these!' Emma put the reins into Leo's hand, closed the gate, and went back to Mississippi. The mare was stretching her neck over the fence, looking uneasy. 'It's all right,' Emma reassured her, stroking her and pulling a burr out of her mane. 'We'll soon be back. Word of honour.'

'Max is right, Emma,' said Leo. 'Riding over to Clipperbush's house is a silly idea. What are you going to do there?'

'See what's what,' replied Emma. She took the reins from the speechless Leo's hand and swung herself up on Aldo's back. 'I'll find out what's going on. Let go of those reins, Max.'

'Won't,' said Max. 'Not unless you take us with you.'

Emma sighed. 'All right. But only one of you. Aldo can't carry all three of us. Who's it to be?'

The two brothers looked at each other.

'We'll toss for it,' said Leo, and he won.

Max was so cross he could almost have stamped on the coin they had tossed, although he was usually rather unwilling to get on a horse.

'Tell Dolly I've gone for a little ride on Aldo with Leo,' Emma said to him. 'But don't say what I'm planning to do, okay?'

'Okay,' grunted Max. 'I'm not stupid.'

'And keep Missie company,' said Emma as she rode through the gateway. 'I think she's a little worried.'

'All right, all right, I'll hold her hand,' muttered Max.

Then he watched enviously as Emma and his brother rode away.

*   *   *

Aldo was not the fastest of horses. He stopped every time a car drove by, and wouldn't trot on until it had disappeared round the next bend. But luckily there were not many cars on the road to Clipperbush's house, and it didn't seem to Emma such a long way as it had on the morning when they had gone to fetch Mississippi.

They tied Aldo up in the little wood behind Clipperbush's house, gave him a few carrots to nibble and then made their way to the big, dark house.

This time there were two cars standing in the yard—the Alligator's big flashy one and an old banger.

102

'Look at that!' whispered Leo as they passed the two vehicles. 'That's Harry's car.'

Emma was making straight for the front door, which she and Dolly had used, but Leo took her round the back to a narrow door at the back of the house.

'It's the way into the kitchen,' he whispered. 'I sometimes used to deliver old Clipperbush's bread, and his housekeeper always brought me this way.'

The kitchen was empty, and as dusty as if no one had cooked anything in it for centuries. Only the fridge was humming away, there were used coffee filters and two empty white wine bottles in the sink, and greasy pizza boxes were stacked on the table.

Leo really did know his way around Clipperbush's house. Without hesitation, he led Emma down long corridors and up a steep staircase to the top floor.

'Clipperbush always used to let me rummage around up here,' he whispered to Emma. 'Sometimes he played at being Tom Sawyer and hunting for treasure with me. He'd hide a cigar box full of fifty-pence pieces somewhere in the house, and I had to look for it. Sometimes it took me all afternoon, and Clipperbush thought it was very funny. He never let me keep the money, though.'

Leo put his ear to a door, opened it a crack, and peered cautiously inside. 'The living room,' he whispered. 'Come on.' He went into the big room, beckoning Emma to follow him. Until now all had been perfectly quiet in the big house, but at this point they suddenly heard voices. Voices in the next room.

Emma recognized one of them at once. It was the Alligator's. Then she recognized the other as well. Leo had been right. Mr Procter's apprentice, Harry, was visiting the Alligator.

'They're in there,' whispered Leo. 'In Clipperbush's study.'

Cautiously, they stole towards the door. It was standing slightly ajar. Emma plucked up all her courage, and peered through the narrow opening.

Leo crouched down and squinted in too.

There stood the two of them, the Alligator smoking a cigarette, and Harry hanging around him like a skinny little dog.

'Are you quite sure no one saw you?' asked the Alligator. 'Not even the vet?'

'Oh, him!' Harry waved the idea away. 'He's always deep in thought—he wouldn't spot an elephant unless he fell over it. Of course, it was bad luck that he came marching through the door just as I was leaving the house. But I'm a fast mover. I ducked down behind the water butt, and the vet just passed and never noticed me. No problem!' He laughed. 'When he came to fetch his car from us later, he was telling me at great length how someone had broken into Dolly Flowerdew's house.'

Clipperbush's nephew nodded, pleased, and flicked his cigarette ash on to the carpet. Then he put out his hand.

'Give it here, then.'

Harry fumbled with the zip fastener

of his anorak. 'Just a minute,' he muttered. 'This is always sticking.'

Albert Gosling snapped his fingers impatiently. 'Come on.'

'Okay, okay!' Harry pulled until the zip came undone. 'It's not a posh jacket like yours.'

He took a folded piece of paper out of his inside pocket and handed it to the Alligator. 'Took me ages to find this thing, you know. Dolly's not all that tidy. I finally found it up on her pin-board in the kitchen.'

Emma knew only too well what it was. The agreement for the sale of Mississippi. Why hadn't they thought of that?

'Wonderful!' Albert Gosling patted Harry's thin shoulder. Then he took a cigarette lighter out of his pocket and held the flame against the paper.

'There we are!' Pleased, he watched as the charred remains of the sale agreement fell on the carpet. 'So now the mare belongs to me. I can't wait to see the expression on that stubborn little girl's stupid face. What a shame! No horse any more, and no money to buy another one.'

Gosling trod out the last glowing remnants with his shiny polished shoes.

Leo groaned slightly. Emma put her finger to her lips—and as she did so, her elbow knocked against the door.

Harry and the Alligator looked round.

In alarm, Emma and Leo sprang back from the half-open door.

'Did you hear that?' asked the Alligator.

At that moment Leo trod on a creaking floorboard.

A couple of strides brought Albert Gosling to the doorway. He pushed the door wide open—and found himself looking at an empty room. Emma was lying under Clipperbush's big sofa, and Leo had hidden behind the curtains at the last moment.

'There was someone in here!' growled the Alligator. 'Go on, Harry, search the room.'

'What, me?' Reluctantly, Harry followed him through the doorway. 'Why me? I've done my work. Give me my money and I'll be off.'

'I said search the place!' the Alligator snapped at him. 'If someone was eavesdropping on us, you're in on this as well.'

Emma could hardly breathe, she had to lie so flat to fit into her hiding place. The broken metal springs of the sofa's upholstery were digging into her back. All the same, she cautiously moved her head slightly forward. She still couldn't see much more than the two men's shoes, but that was better than nothing.

'Okay,' grunted Harry. 'Where do I start?'

'Anywhere you like, idiot,' said the Alligator. 'Just get moving, that's all, and I'll keep an eye on the door.'

Harry muttered something that Emma couldn't make out, turned—and made for the sofa.

Emma's heart was thudding. Now what? She desperately slid back as far as she possibly could.

Then she suddenly heard Leo's voice.

'Hello, Harry!' he said. 'What are you doing here?'

Emma almost let out a cry of shock,

but she just managed to bite her lip. With bated breath, she pushed herself far enough forward to see Leo's trainers. Right in front of the sofa—so close that she could have touched them if she'd put out her hand. For a few endless moments all was perfectly quiet.

Then the Alligator said, in a dangerously calm voice, 'That's the very question I'd like to ask you, boy.' His shiny shoes took a step in Leo's direction. 'Just what are you doing in my house? Hold him tight, Harry.'

'It's only Leo,' Emma heard Harry saying. 'The baker's son.'

'Well, what *are* you doing here?' snapped the Alligator. 'You're trespassing on my property, did you know that?'

'It was for a bet!' replied Leo. He could always think up excuses at the speed of light.

'What kind of a bet?' asked Gosling.

'Hey!' Leo trod on Harry's foot. 'Take your greasy hands off me! I'm not going to run away.'

'You'd better not try it,' said the

Alligator. 'I'd be delighted to hand you over to the police.'

But that's what you certainly won't do, you nasty man, thought Emma. The police are just about the last people you want coming here. And Leo knew it too.

'Look, I was only having a bet with my brother,' said Leo. 'I bet him I could get in here even though you're living in the house. My brother is always showing off, so I wanted to get one over on him.'

'It's a fact, his brother really is always showing off,' said Harry.

'Oh yes?' The Alligator still sounded suspicious. 'And how are you going to prove that you got in here? Is your precious brother standing outside casing the joint?'

'Don't be so silly!' Leo stepped nervously from foot to foot. 'He'd never dare come into the yard here. On account of Clipperbush's ghost, know what I mean? No, I have to bring him one of Clipperbush's ballpoint pens as proof. One of those with his name on them. They're lying around all over the place here. Look, I'd picked one up already. There, you see!'

Emma could hardly take all this in. How could anyone make up such a clever pack of lies?

'It's true!' Harry looked positively relieved. 'He does have one. Well, I guess we can let him go, can't we?'

'Hm.' The Alligator obviously wasn't entirely convinced. Emma's nose was beginning to tickle. She quickly pinched it. 'Are there any more of your sort sneaking around the place here?' That was the Alligator again.

'No, honest!' Leo sounded perfectly truthful. 'Not that I know of. Can I go now?'

There was another moment's silence.

'How long have you been in this room?' growled Albert Gosling. 'Were you eavesdropping on us?'

'Why would I want to eavesdrop on you?' asked Leo. 'I suddenly heard voices, and I thought it was old Clipperbush's ghost. So of course I hid at once. I bet you'd have done the same.'

111

'Maybe.' The Alligator took another step in Leo's direction. He was right in front of him now. 'But I'll just say this: if you did overhear anything, forget it. And forget it very fast, get it?'

'I didn't overhear a thing!' said Leo. 'Word of honour.'

'Just as well for you.' Albert Gosling stepped back again. 'All the same, Harry will be keeping an eye on you in future. Won't you, Harry?'

'Yeah,' muttered Harry. He didn't sound very enthusiastic about this prospect.

'Take the boy outside,' said the Alligator. 'And give him a good kick up the backside to help him find his way home faster.'

Harry disappeared with Leo, and Emma was left alone with the Alligator.

Her left arm was itching like mad, but she dared not scratch it. She lay there perfectly still. The dusty carpet tickled her nose. She heard the Alligator lighting a cigarette. Then his shoes came closer, and he sat down on the sofa.

Emma gritted her teeth as the springs pressed down even harder on her back. But she didn't utter a sound. The Alligator would never believe that *she* was here because of a bet as well.

He crossed his legs. Cigarette ash fell on the carpet.

If I have to lie here much longer, thought Emma, I shall go mad. Stark staring mad.

Then Harry came back. Without Leo.

'Now what?' he asked. 'Do I get my money yet?'

'It's in the car,' said the Alligator, standing up. Relieved, Emma gasped for air.

'What are you going to do next?' asked Harry. The two of them were walking towards the door.

'My lawyer is already waiting at the station,' said Gosling. 'I'm going to pick him up, and then we'll call on Daffy Dolly. The horse will be back in my stable this evening.'

'Well, have fun,' said Harry. 'Dolly's not going to be pleased.'

The Alligator laughed. 'There's

nothing she can do about it. And the best of it is, she'll think she lost the sale agreement herself.'

Then the two of them were gone. Emma heard them going downstairs, but she dared not come out of hiding until she heard the car engines start down in the yard.

With her nose itching and her back aching, she crawled out from under the sofa. Then she ran as fast as she could, out of that horrible house, across the empty yard, and back to Aldo.

*   *   *

Leo was already waiting for her.

He was sitting on the grass beside Aldo, whittling a piece of wood with his penknife. Emma went over to him and gave him a kiss. A big kiss.

'Thank you!' she said. 'Thank you for saving me from the Alligator. That's the most wonderful thing anyone has ever done for me.'

Leo almost cut his finger and turned red as a beetroot. 'Don't mention it,' he muttered. 'It was only natural.'

'Only natural? Did you hear that, Aldo?' Emma took Leo's hand and pulled him to his feet. 'You were like a hero. A genuine hero! I'd never have dared do a thing like that, not in a thousand years. I thought my heart had dropped right down into my boots. If that man had seen me, then . . .'

The mere idea still left Emma speechless.

'Well, that was it.' Leo shrugged his shoulders and put his knife away. 'We had to make sure he *didn't* see you. He'd never have let you go so easily.'

'You know something?' Emma pushed him in the direction of Aldo. 'Your brother would show off for about a hundred years over doing something like that. And you act like it was something to be ashamed of. Come on, get up on Aldo. We must be back before that man comes to take Mississippi away.'

She took hold of Aldo's mane and swung herself up on him. Leo scrambled up and held on as he sat behind her.

'But there's nothing you can do

about it,' he said. 'He'll simply say that he just left Mississippi with Dolly at livery for a little while, now that you don't have the sale agreement any more.'

'Well, as a matter of fact I do, so that's too bad,' said Emma as they made for the road. 'Come on, fatso!' she said, trying to make the gelding go faster. 'Get a move on or your friend Mississippi will soon be dog food.'

Aldo pricked up his ears, and he actually did get a move on.

'What? I don't understand!' complained Leo. 'What did the Alligator burn, then?'

'The sale agreement,' said Emma. 'But I kept a copy.'

*   *   *

When Aldo finally trotted through Dolly's gate, Albert Gosling's car was already standing outside the house. With a horsebox attached to it.

Emma and Leo jumped down from Aldo's back.

'Hey, where have you been?' Max

called to them. 'You've no idea of the trouble that's been going on here.'

'We know!' said Emma, pressing Aldo's reins into his hand. 'Here, take him to the paddock, will you? Leo, tell Dolly I'll be with her in a minute, and she's not to let Mississippi go, okay?'

Leo nodded. Max looked from one of them to the other, baffled.

'Come on, tell me! What happened?' he asked. 'What did you find out?'

But Emma was already on her way to the house.

She charged upstairs to her room, snatched her rucksack out of the cupboard and fished out the copy of the sales agreement.

When she reached the horses' paddock, breathless, the Alligator was already trying to pull Mississippi out of her field by her halter. The mare was tossing her head, her feet planted, and looking around uneasily, while Dolly, waving a pitchfork about, was talking earnestly to a small, fat man in glasses.

Max and Leo had placed Aldo across the gateway, blocking the Alligator's way out.

'Stop!' called Emma. 'Stop! That's my horse!'

She slipped past Aldo and hurried over to Dolly and the little man. They all looked at her in surprise. Mississippi snorted, and pulled against her halter so hard that Albert Gosling could hardly hold her.

'I have a copy!" cried Emma. 'I have a copy of the sale agreement.'

Suddenly it was perfectly quiet. Only the horses stamped uneasily on the spot.

The Alligator looked at her as if he would snap her in half.

The little man nervously adjusted his glasses. 'May I see the copy, please?' he asked.

Emma handed him the precious piece of paper. Frowning, the man read the agreement, studied the signature, and gave the sheet of paper back to Emma. 'Excuse me, please,' he murmured. Then he quickly went over to Albert Gosling and talked to him.

He looked rather annoyed.

'That's Clipperbush's nephew's lawyer,' Dolly whispered to Emma.

'The two of them turned up fifteen minutes ago wanting to see the sale agreement for Mississippi. And do you know what?'

'It had gone,' said Emma.

'Exactly!' Dolly looked at her in surprise. 'But how did you know? I must have mislaid it. I searched frantically while that horrible man was getting the halter down. Luckily Mississippi wasn't easy to catch, or they'd have gone off with her by now.'

'You didn't mislay it,' Emma interrupted her.

The lawyer and the Alligator were still talking to each other, while Mississippi tugged at her halter and fidgeted anxiously, looking at Emma.

'What?' Dolly took hold of Emma's arm. 'What did you say?'

'You didn't mislay it,' Emma repeated. 'Gosling got Harry to steal it for him. You did lock the door when we went shopping.'

Her grandmother just looked at her, speechless.

'Can you prove that?' she asked quietly.

Emma shook her head. 'Not unless the police believe Leo and me more than they believe Harry and Gosling. Because we saw them burning the agreement.'

The lawyer came back to them.

'Excuse me, Mrs Flowerdew,' he said, 'but I have told my client that this copy of the agreement naturally changes the situation entirely, and I have strongly advised him to reconsider his present mode of conduct.'

'What does all that mean?' asked Emma.

'It means,' said the little man, pushing the knot of his tie further up, 'it means that the horse stays in your possession for the time being, and my client will drop his claim.'

'Good,' said Emma.

Looking grim, she went up to the Alligator, snatched the lead rope from his hand and led Missie back to the paddock. The mare nudged Emma's shoulder with her nose and lovingly nibbled her sweater. Emma took off the halter, flung her arms around her and pressed her face to the horse's neck.

'That was a close thing!' she whispered. 'Oh, Missie, do you realize what a close thing it was?'

Mississippi stepped restlessly aside, shook her mane, and looked enquiringly down at Emma. Emma pulled the mare's head down to her and scratched behind her ears.

'That man will never get you,' she whispered. 'Even if I have to run away to America with you. He'll never, ever get you.'

When Max saw that Emma had taken Mississippi back to the paddock, he led Aldo back to the field as well. As for Leo, he strolled past the Alligator grinning at him.

'You again?' Albert Gosling's eyes almost popped out of his head with rage when he recognized Leo. 'I see. You wait, you lying little runt. If I ever get my hands on you again, then I'll . . .'

'Then you'll what?' asked Dolly, placing herself firmly between the two of them. She was still holding the pitchfork. 'Aren't you content with

121

coming here and trying to steal a horse? Do you have to threaten children as well? Not in my back yard, you don't.' She whistled, and Shaggy bounded across the grass, breathing heavily.

'Shaggy!' Dolly pointed to Albert Gosling. 'Take that away. Off you go.'

Shaggy trotted over to the Alligator, grabbed his sleeve with gentle pressure of his teeth, and pulled him towards the road.

'Tell this monster to let go of me at once!' Gosling shouted over his shoulder. 'I'm sure you can't pay for the damage to my suit.'

'I don't intend to,' replied Dolly.

Albert Gosling cursed and swore in such a loud voice that Lizzie Dockfoot next door leaned out of her attic window. But Shaggy just went on pulling him away.

'Well, I'll be off,' said Gosling's lawyer, with a nervous smile. 'Forgive us for disturbing you, Mrs Flowerdew.'

Emma carefully closed the paddock gate and stood beside Dolly. Shaggy was just pulling the Alligator out of the gate. But he didn't let go of his sleeve until they reached the pavement. Right next to Dolly's dustbin.

'When did Shaggy learn to do that?' asked Max.

'Exactly.' Emma shook her head incredulously. 'He usually just barks.'

'He still does that,' said Dolly. 'But I've noticed that he likes carrying things about. For instance, taking bags to put them in the rubbish bins. You just have to tell him, "Take that away", and he picks up whatever you point to and goes off with it. Useful, don't you think?'

'Well, he had a huge bag of rubbish to take away this time,' said Max. 'And now maybe someone can tell me what happened at Clipperbush's house.'

'Clipperbush's house?' Surprised, Dolly looked first at Emma and then at Leo. 'Aha. So that's where your little ride through the woods on Aldo took you.'

'Well, yes.' Embarrassed, Emma drew circles in the sand with the toe of her shoe. 'We thought we'd see what was going on.'

'Ah.' Dolly frowned. 'Is that why Gosling was foaming at the mouth when he set eyes on Leo?'

Emma nodded. 'Leo rescued me.' She looked at Max. 'Your brother's a hero. A real hero.'

Leo didn't know where to look.

CHAPTER 12

'Well, what an adventurous story,' said Mr Knapp. 'Adventurous and rather alarming.'

Dolly had phoned him right after that afternoon's events, but he had been in a pigsty at the time. And after that he had to treat three cows, an old horse and a sheep. By the time he was finally sitting at the living-room table with Emma and Dolly, it was already getting dark outside.

'Do you think Gosling will come back again?' asked Emma.

The vet stirred his coffee thoughtfully. Emma had made him a particularly strong cup. 'You must take good care of that copy of the agreement, anyway,' he said. 'If that fellow will put someone up to committing burglary for him, then he really must want Mississippi back a great deal.'

'But why?' Dolly put a cloth over the budgies' cage and sat down on the sofa beside Shaggy. 'Why would he suddenly go taking such risks for a horse he was going to send to the knacker only a few days ago?'

'It must be something to do with his inheritance,' said Mr Knapp. 'Even if he's trying to make us think he's suffering a guilty conscience over his dead uncle. No, his inheritance is at risk. And we have to find out why very fast indeed. Dolly,' he said, putting his coffee down, 'pass me the telephone, would you?'

Dolly rose to her feet and put the phone down on the table in front of Knapp. The vet took a small booklet out of his jacket pocket, leafed through it for a moment and then picked up the receiver.

'Cross your fingers!' he whispered.

Emma looked enquiringly at Dolly, but she just shrugged her shoulders.

'Hello?' said Mr Knapp. 'Is that Mrs Strettle? Yes, good evening, this is Knapp the vet speaking. I'm sorry to disturb you so late, but could you call in at my surgery tomorrow morning with your Barnabas? There's a nasty strain of dog flu going around locally at the moment, and I thought—no, no, not life-threatening, but—yes, yes, yes, there is indeed an inoculation he can have, that's why I—yes, yes, we can do it tomorrow morning. Fine. Around eleven? Don't mention it. All part of the service, Mrs Strettle. Yes, see you tomorrow, then. Have a nice evening.'

Sighing, the vet put the receiver down.

'Knapp!' said Dolly. 'What a shameless liar you are! Dog flu, indeed! And you're not even blushing. People ought to be careful of you.'

Emma looked at the two of them, baffled. 'What was that all about?' she asked. 'Who's Mrs Strettle?'

'Dora Strettle,' said Dolly, pouring herself more coffee, 'Dora Strettle, dear heart, was John Clipperbush's housekeeper for fifteen years. Since his death I think she's retired, and she spends her time feeding chocolates to her dog and circulating rumours about Clipperbush's will.'

Mr Knapp nodded. 'Exactly. And we have to look closely at those rumours. That's the only way we can find out why Clipperbush's nephew has suddenly discovered his conscience.'

'Oh, I see. So there isn't any dog flu going around?' Emma looked admiringly at the vet. 'The way you told the story I'd have fallen for it myself.'

'Really?' The vet smiled, flattered.

'Look at the man, will you?' cried Dolly. 'Now he prides himself on being a good liar too.'

'Only for the best,' said Knapp. He looked at Emma. 'Do you still want to train as a vet?'

'You bet I do!' replied Emma. 'Why?'

'Because you're going to assist me tomorrow. Surgery hours begin at nine, so you should be there at a quarter to.

Then I can explain a little of what it's all about to my real assistant before we start. All right?'

Emma was speechless.

'Does that mean yes?' asked Knapp.

'I . . .' Emma swallowed. 'I don't think I can do it.'

'Of course you can do it,' said the vet, and he pushed his mug over to her. 'A girl who makes such good coffee can do anything. Will you pour me another?'

CHAPTER 13

Mr Knapp lived and worked in a big old house that stood all by itself on the main road among the woods and meadows. The people of four villages brought their animals to him, and the vet drove out to the local farms to treat sick cows, pigs and horses.

When Dolly dropped Emma at his place at quarter to nine on the dot, there were already four people in the waiting room: two women with their cats, a man with a boxer dog, and another man with a little goat kid on his lap. They looked distrustfully at Emma as she went through to the surgery.

'Ah, my new assistant!' Mr Knapp welcomed her in. 'Put this white coat on, will you? Louisa, my practice nurse, will come in a moment and show you the ropes. I told her you'd be making the coffee today. Louisa's coffee,' added the vet, lowering his voice, 'Louisa's coffee is as thin as dishwater.'

Emma grinned. 'That's okay,' she said. Then, with her heart thudding, she put on the white coat, which was much too big for her, rolled up the sleeves and waited.

Louisa had dyed red hair and big earrings, and looked very nice. She showed Emma where the anaesthetics and the disinfectants were kept, where she could find dog biscuits to keep the patients calm, which scissors to use to cut up bandages, how many different kinds of ear drops there were for animals—and where the coffee machine stood. Then she waved to

Emma and left her in charge.

'Ready?' asked Mr Knapp. 'Then call the first patient in.'

Emma adjusted her white coat and opened the door.

'Next, please!' she called to the people in the waiting room.

The man with the little goat stood up.

*   *   *

During the next two hours Emma called, 'Next, please!' exactly fifteen times. She helped Mr Knapp to bind up dogs' paws, she stroked the heads of cats to reassure them, she opened birdcages and pet carriers, and she fetched dressings. She had to ask Louisa for help only twice.

At nearly eleven o'clock Mr Knapp led Emma into the little room next to his treatment surgery, where his coffee machine and his desk stood.

'Mrs Strettle is sitting in the waiting room,' he said in a low voice. 'I've told Louisa that we certainly won't be needing her help with this particular patient, and she might as well take a break. She'd be bound to notice our little white lie about the dog flu inoculation. You've been helping me so well all morning that you'd be fine with this one on your own anyway. But make sure you don't say too much, won't you? Right, remember: we've already seen fifteen cases of this strain of flu, but Mrs Strettle's pet only needs to have some drops of a special brown liquid on his dog biscuits to be protected from it. All right?'

Emma nodded.

Knapp took a little bottle of brown fluid out of the pocket of his coat and handed it to her. 'These are harmless vitamin drops. You'll be putting four of them on one of the dog biscuits we usually give the patients as a treat. Make it all really tense and exciting. Meanwhile I'll try to get a conversation going. When Mrs Strettle's dog has eaten his biscuit, I'll make a great business of examining him, and try asking her more questions as I do it. And if a good question occurs to you, then ask it. And listen carefully to everything she says. Okay?'

Emma nodded again.

They went back to the treatment room together.

'Here we go then!' the vet whispered to her. 'Wish us luck!'

Emma opened the waiting-room door. 'Next, please,' she called.

A sturdy elderly lady got up and pushed her way past Emma into the treatment room. She was carrying a dog as long as it was wide.

'Quick, Mr Knapp!' she cried. 'Quick, inoculate him. Who knows, one of those other dogs in the waiting room may have infected him already!' She put the dog on the examining table and felt his nose, which looked as if someone had squashed it flat. There was a worried expression on her face.

'It's warm!' cried Mrs Strettle. 'Feel that! Warm! And first thing this morning it was nicely cool and damp.'

'Now, now, Mrs Strettle, don't upset yourself.' Mr Knapp gently pushed her aside. 'Infection doesn't show as quickly as that with this strain of flu. My assistant is going to prepare a biscuit for Barnabas to eat, and then he'll be perfectly safe from this particular infection.'

'Assistant?' Mrs Strettle watched suspiciously as Emma let four of the brown drops fall on the dog biscuit. 'But she's a child. Where's Louisa?'

'Oh, she's in the next room,' said Mr Knapp, 'but don't worry, Emma is very good at the job. Today we've already—' He looked up. 'Emma, how many dogs have we already immunized against this strain of flu today?'

'Eleven,' said Emma.

She put the dog biscuit on a saucer and carried it over to the examining table. Mrs Strettle's dog sniffed at it with interest, and then ate it in a single gulp.

'Oh, what a clever dog!' said Emma. 'Anyone can see that right away! What's his name?'

'Barnabas!' said Mrs Strettle, sniffing. 'He's the cleverest dog there ever was.' She brought a tissue out of her handbag and blew her nose. 'Dear me, I have such a shocking cold. Do you think some drops like that would do me good as well? I just can't shake this cold off.'

'Where did you catch it?' asked the vet, giving the empty saucer back to Emma.

Mrs Strettle sighed. 'Oh, at a funeral. Funerals in the pouring rain ought not to be allowed.'

She sneezed.

'Funeral?' said Mr Knapp. 'Not John Clipperbush's funeral?'

'No, no!' Mrs Strettle patted Barnabas's fat back. 'The weather for *his* funeral was kind. Mr Clipperbush always knew what was right and proper. It was a dog's funeral. My best friend's dachshund had died.'

'Ah, I see.' Mr Knapp cast Emma a disappointed glance, and put the earpieces of his stethoscope in his ears. 'Since you're here, Mrs Strettle, I might as well give Barnabas a thorough looking-over. Is that all right?'

'Of course.' Mrs Strettle was examining Emma from head to foot. 'This girl really isn't at all bad at helping you out, Mr Knapp. What do you want to be when you grow up, dear? Are you planning to be a vet yourself?'

'Yes, that's right,' said Emma. 'What do you do?'

'Me?' Mrs Strettle laughed. 'Oh, I never got further than being a housekeeper.'

'Mrs Strettle used to work for old Mr Clipperbush, Emma,' said the vet.

'Oh, him!' cried Emma. 'The owner of the horse. Do you know his nephew too?'

'Yes, of course.' Mrs Strettle found the next tissue in her bag. 'A nice man. So well groomed and somehow— energetic, yes, that's the word for it. When Mr Clipperbush died he dropped in to give me a bunch of flowers, and he asked whether I'd like to go on working for him if it turned out he had inherited the farm, but I said no. I've done enough working in my life. Now all I want to do is look after Barnabas.'

Emma and the vet exchanged a quick glance.

'Oh, really?' Mr Knapp was looking at Barnabas's teeth now. When

Barnabas began to growl, he quickly closed the dog's muzzle again. 'Maybe you'll be thinking it over, all the same. This man Gosling will need help if he inherits such a large property.'

Mrs Strettle smiled, in a way that suggested she knew a little more than other people.

'Yes, *if*,' she said. 'I think there's going to be a little surprise about that.'

She blew her nose.

'What kind of surprise?' asked Mr Knapp.

Mrs Strettle shook her head. 'No, I really can't tell you any more about it.'

'But you told the Alligator!' said Emma.

It had slipped out just like that. She hadn't meant to say anything. Horrified, Emma pressed her lips together, but of course it was much too late for that.

Mr Knapp sighed—and started examining Barnabas's ears. Mrs Strettle looked at Emma in astonishment. 'Who on earth is the Alligator?' she asked.

'Albert Gosling,' muttered Emma,

without looking at her. 'Clipperbush's nephew.'

Mrs Strettle went red in the face and buried her nose in her tissue. Mr Knapp gave Barnabas a few little dog treats and looked at his owner. 'Did you really tell him anything about the will?' he asked.

Mrs Strettle was still sniffing into her tissue.

'Dora!' said Mr Knapp. 'Have you told John Clipperbush's nephew anything about his uncle's will?'

'Well, yes!' Mrs Strettle dabbed at her red nose. 'Yes, I have. When he was there on my doorstep for the third time, with another beautiful bouquet of flowers, you know, the kind with cellophane round it, asking if I would go and work for him. Then I told him, so that he wouldn't go on spending all that money on flowers for nothing, and he'd go away and leave me alone.'

'*What* did you tell him?' asked Mr Knapp in his strictest voice.

Emma held her breath.

'I told him he'd made a big mistake,' muttered Mrs Strettle.

'What mistake?'

Mrs Strettle straightened Barnabas's red collar. 'Selling Clipperbush's mare. To Dolores Flowerdew. You know, the woman with all those animals. I wouldn't think of such a thing for Barnabas. He has me all to himself.'

'But,' said Mr Knapp, beginning to lose patience, 'but what, for heaven's sake, was so bad about Clipperbush's nephew selling the mare?'

Mrs Strettle looked at him crossly. 'I really don't know why I should tell you too, Mr Knapp.'

Knapp sighed. He picked fat Barnabas up and put him down on the floor.

'Dora,' he said, 'let me introduce you to Dolly Flowerdew's granddaughter. This is Emma. She is the new owner of Clipperbush's mare, and for the last few days Albert Gosling has been doing all he can to get the horse back from her. Please tell us why!'

Mrs Strettle frowned. 'Oh, dear me!' she moaned. 'I wasn't to know that!'

She found a new tissue and blew her

nose again. Then she looked at Emma.

'He'll lose his inheritance, that's why,' she said. 'If he doesn't have that horse he goes away empty-handed.'

Barnabas snuffled at Emma's shoe with interest and then licked it.

'Are you sure, Dora?' asked the vet. 'Absolutely sure?'

'It's in Mr Clipperbush's will.' Mrs Strettle lowered her voice and looked in all directions, as if afraid she might see old Clipperbush's ghost in one of the cupboards of medicaments. 'I saw it while I was going round with the vacuum cleaner. It was lying on his desk, and I took a look at it. Not many people can read his scrawl, but I can. I've had to decipher his shopping lists often enough. It said: "I, John Clipperbush, being in full possession of my mental powers, do hereby leave to my nephew Albert Gosling all my landed property in the village of Anderham, to wit the house and furniture, the stables and the land belonging to the house, as well as my mare Mississippi, but on one condition: he must never sell the horse, and must have Mississippi cared for to the best of his ability until her natural death, which, it is to be hoped, will not be for a long time. If he does not keep the horse, the farm and all its land will go to the RSPCA in Neddlestead." That's what it said, word for word.' Mrs Strettle smiled. 'I have a very good memory.'

'Heavens above!' groaned Mr Knapp. 'No wonder the man doesn't shrink from a little burglary! But what about Clipperbush's money?'

Mrs Strettle picked Barnabas up and kissed him on top of his fat head. 'His nephew asked me about that too, but I really don't know the answer. Old Clipperbush drew it out of his bank not long before his death, and then it disappeared.' She sneezed again. 'Poor Mr Gosling. He had such wonderful plans for the old farm. He was going to build some semi-detached houses on the land and a fur farm, you know, for breeding animals you put around your neck as a collar. Anyone can understand why he felt terrible about not being able to do all that, don't you

140

agree? Just because of that stupid old horse.' She blew her nose once more and looked at Mr Knapp. 'Oh, please do give me some of those brown drops to put on a biscuit as well! They might do this cold good.'

But Mr Knapp was gently propelling her towards the door.

'Certainly not!' he said. 'All they do to humans is make you itch. Good day to you, Mrs Strettle.'

CHAPTER 14

After that nothing happened for a week. The Alligator went back to town. Harry was off work sick. The copy of the sale agreement for Mississippi was locked in Mr Knapp's medicine cupboard, and Emma and the dogs had taken to sleeping in the stable every night. Dolly was not too keen on that, but she didn't actually forbid it. And before she got on her bike every morning she brought a mug of hot cocoa out to the stable for Emma.

Then, a week after Mrs Strettle's confession, a letter came for Dolly from the District Court.

'Well, listen to this,' said Dolly, leaning over the fence of the paddock, where Emma was grooming the horses and pulling burrs out of their manes and tails. 'I've been asked to the reading of John Clipperbush's will. What do you think of that?'

Emma lowered her brush in surprise. Mississippi turned her head and started nibbling her sweater.

'Does that mean you've inherited something from him?'

Dolly shrugged her shoulders. 'I suppose so. John sometimes said that if I survived him he'd leave me his books. But I thought he was only joking.' Thoughtfully, she folded up the letter again and put it back in the envelope.

'Dolly,' said Emma, picking some straw out of Mississippi's mane, 'why didn't you want to go to America when you had the chance?'

Her grandmother smiled. 'Oh, I'd have been happy to go to America. But

142

not with John Clipperbush, you see. Now let's drop the subject. You go on grooming the horses and I'll see to the dogs. Shaggy is bound to be chewing up my rugs again, and I haven't seen Tom and Jerry since breakfast. They're probably digging up Lizzie's rose beds.' She began strolling slowly back towards the house. 'Oh, and by the way,' she called over her shoulder, 'the will is going to be read in four days' time. So after that I don't suppose we'll have to wonder what that man Gosling is up to any more, and you can sleep in your bed at night.'

'Oh, I don't care about that!' Emma called back. 'I like sleeping in the stable, even if there are rats.'

*   *   *

Dolly and Emma spent the rest of the morning mucking out the stables, scrubbing the chickens' perches and the feed and water buckets, getting fifteen ticks out of Shaggy's coat, patching up two of the cats that had scratched each other, and catching four

143

hens who had wandered off into Lizzie Dockfoot's cabbage patch.

In the afternoon Emma went for a long walk in the woods with Mississippi, and then she had a picnic with Leo and Max on the grass in front of the house. Shaggy lay down beside them and made sure that not a crumb was wasted. The little white cat jumped on Emma's lap to be stroked. Only Tom and Jerry didn't come to join in the picnic. When the two dogs did not turn up for their supper either, Dolly began to worry about them. She even drove her car a little way down the road, but she came back on her own.

At nine in the evening, when Emma went to the garden gate again to call Tom and Jerry, she found the letter. It was stuck into the letter box.

There was no stamp on the envelope, and it didn't say who the sender was. Dolly's address had been typed on the envelope.

That's funny, thought Emma—and she took the envelope into the house. Dolly was sitting on the living-room sofa, reading.

'There's another letter for you,' said Emma. 'But it doesn't say on the envelope who it's from.'

Surprised, Dolly looked up. 'What kind of a letter comes at this time of day?' She opened the envelope. There was a neatly folded sheet of paper inside it.

Dolly unfolded it and read it. Then she handed it to Emma without a word.

The typed letter said:

```
If you want to see your
dogs again, then come
alone to the Clipperbush
farm the day after
tomorrow, at six p.m.
prompt, bringing with you
the following: this
letter, the sales
agreement for the mare
Mississippi, and the mare
herself. In addition you
are to tell everyone that
you find the horse too
expensive to keep, and
that you therefore,
```

although with regret,
have taken it back to the
Clipperbush farm. If you
carry out all these
conditions, you will get
your dogs back again
three days after John
Clipperbush's will has
been executed.

A dog-lover

'A blackmail letter!' whispered Emma. 'This is a real blackmail letter.' She looked incredulously at her grandmother. 'Now what do we do?'

Dolly shrugged her shoulders. 'I've no idea. I've seen this kind of thing thousands of times on TV, but I'd never have thought I might get a horrible thing like that myself. After all, blackmail is usually about money, and I don't have much of that.'

'But this is about Mississippi,' said Emma.

Dolly nodded. 'And Tom and Jerry. Oh, for goodness' sake, why can't those dogs look after themselves better? I shouldn't be surprised if a sausage was enough to lure them both into the kidnapper's car. They probably got in entirely of their own accord. I wouldn't put that past them.'

Emma suddenly felt weak at the knees. She sat down on Dolly's sofa.

'Maybe we ought to call the police,' she said quietly.

But Dolly shook her head. 'Heavens, no. You don't know the local policeman here, but I do. He's seen too many American crime films on television, and he's terrified of dogs. No, we have to deal with this by ourselves. I just wish I knew how.'

Emma couldn't remember ever having seen Dolly's face look so tired. She picked the letter up from the table and read it again.

'We could go to Clipperbush's house and search it,' she suggested. 'Leo showed me the back door. We could take Shaggy with us, he'd be sure to find them.'

But Dolly shook her head.

'Forget it, darling,' she said. 'That man isn't stupid. He certainly didn't kidnap the dogs himself, and very certainly he's not keeping them in his house.'

Emma hung her head.

Sighing, Dolly stood up. 'I'll call Knapp. Maybe he can think of something.'

'I know what's going to happen,' said Emma. 'I'll have to give up Mississippi. And then she'll have to go back to that horrible man, and he won't pat her or talk to her and he won't let her out to graze. He'll put her in his stable until he has his silly money, and then she'll die of loneliness. That's what's going to happen.'

'No, it isn't!' said Dolly, picking up the phone. 'I promise you it isn't. Even if I have to get Mississippi back from Clipperbush's stable personally. But now I'm going to call Knapp. You go out to the stable to see Mississippi and stroke her nose. That'll do you more good than if you sit around here thinking gloomy thoughts.'

CHAPTER 15

All was quiet in the stable. Nothing rustled in the straw; the moonlight spun silver threads in the darkness. But Emma couldn't sleep. She tossed and turned restlessly from side to side. Mississippi stood dozing in her box, snorting softly as she slept.

Poor Missie, thought Emma. She doesn't know anything about that letter. Shaggy was smacking his lips in his sleep beside her. Emma buried her face in his coat, but the tears came all the same. What could she do?

Her head hurt with thinking. But no bright ideas came to her. None at all. She couldn't even run away with Missie. She didn't like to think what would happen to Tom and Jerry then. Were there knackers who bought up dogs? Emma rested her head on Shaggy's back.

The big dog whined softly, and his paws twitched restlessly back and forth. Was he dreaming of rabbits?

Hunting? And what do horses dream of?

Emma sat up and looked at the moon through one of the stable windows.

I'd like to be up there, she thought. Far, far away from all these horrible things.

Mississippi snorted.

Emma pushed her blanket aside and went barefoot into the mare's box. The straw prickled her toes. Emma leaned against the partition wall of the box and just stood there looking at Mississippi.

To think that horses sleep standing up! Emma never used to believe it, until she found Aldo doing it in his stable one night. Mr Knapp had tried to explain it to her.

'It's like this,' he had said. 'Horses are among the animals whose only chance when they're in danger is flight. If they lay down to sleep, and a fierce beast of prey came prowling up, it would take far too much time for them to get on their feet. A horse's body would need a few moments to get its sense of balance back. Valuable time would be lost. That's why lying down is a dangerous position for horses.'

Emma leaned her head on the rough wood.

'Oh, Missie,' she murmured. 'Running away from the Alligator won't help.'

Running away wouldn't help at all any more. Not with all those fences and roads. If a horse doesn't come across friendly people, maybe that's just bad luck. It spends its life standing in some musty stable, at best being taken out for someone to ride it occasionally. It has to do what its human owner wants. It's there just for the owner's pleasure.

Emma was startled out of these gloomy thoughts when Shaggy jumped up and ran to the stable door, wagging his tail. Dolly put her head around the door.

'Can't you two sleep either?'

She made her way in with two steaming mugs. She was wearing her thick dressing gown and a pair of rubber boots.

'Shaggy's been sleeping like a baby,'

151

said Emma. 'Sometimes I'd like to be a dog. They don't know about anything.'

'Who can be sure of that?' said Dolly. She sat down on Emma's blanket and patted the place beside her. 'Come along, sit down with me. I've made us hot milk and honey. That doesn't drive gloomy thoughts away, of course, but it does make you feel sleepy. Or so they say.'

Emma sat down beside her grandmother and leaned her head on her shoulder.

'What are we going to do?' she asked.

Dolly shrugged her shoulders.

'I don't know. I've been sitting in the living room all this time wondering that. But I just can't think of anything. I'm afraid we can't do anything until we have the dogs back.' She stroked Emma's hair. 'You know, the one good thing about Clipperbush's stupid will is that his nephew can't let Mississippi be slaughtered now. And I expect that was Clipperbush's intention. Although I do think he might have thought up some cleverer solution to the problem.'

Emma sighed. She sat up and drank her hot milk. 'I don't suppose Mr Knapp can think of anything either, can he?'

Dolly shook her head. 'I'm afraid the poor man is lying in his bed now and having the same trouble as us in getting to sleep. I ought not to have phoned him until tomorrow morning.'

Emma yawned. Shaggy lay down beside her and licked her bare feet.

'Yuk, Shaggy!' Giggling, Emma tucked her feet under her nightie. 'Don't do that, it tickles!'

'That's nothing for Shaggy,' said Dolly, standing up. 'Sometimes he even nibbles between my toes with his teeth. Very carefully, but it's a weird feeling.'

'I think he understands what we're saying,' said Emma. 'Look at him.'

The big dog was gazing at Emma as if he had been mortally insulted.

'Oh, he always looks at people like that,' said Dolly. 'He wants something to eat, as usual. But I'm going back to bed, or I'll be falling off my bike in the morning. Do you think you can get a little sleep now?'

'I'll try.' Emma crawled under her blanket and pulled it up to her chin. 'See you in the morning.'

'See you in the morning,' said Dolly.

By the time she quietly closed the stable door after her, Emma was fast asleep.

CHAPTER 16

Another letter came the next day.

Once again it was in the letter box, along with a postcard from Emma's parents.

Emma found it when she went to look for the post before breakfast. At first she thought nothing of it. Dolly's address was handwritten. In rather scrawly letters, but she could just about make them out. That must be from Alma, thought Emma. Alma did see Dolly regularly, but she was an enthusiastic letter-writer. Then Emma noticed that once again there was no sender's address on the envelope. And no stamp either.

Alarmed, she ran indoors.

Dolly was sitting at the table, reading the newspaper.

'Here,' said Emma, putting the envelope on the table. 'Another of those funny letters without a stamp.'

Dolly put the newspaper down and slit the envelope open with the bread knife.

'Oh dear, this is getting stranger all the time!' she murmured. 'Someone seems to have seen a few too many crime thrillers. Look at that.' She handed Emma the letter. It wasn't either typed or handwritten this time. The text was made of snippets of newsprint stuck together, so that it looked like a blackmail letter from some stupid TV film.

Come to the fishermen's hut by the pool in the woods at one a.m. Come alone and you will get something back that belongs to you.

Emma stared at Dolly. 'What does *this* one mean?'

Her grandmother sighed. 'I don't know. All I know is that I'm going to phone Henrietta and Alma now and put them off. I really don't have the heart to play cards today.'

Dolly was just on her way to the telephone when the kitchen door opened.

'Ah, there you both are!' Mr Knapp ducked under the top of the doorway and came in. 'I'd have come sooner, but I had three cows and a pig to treat this morning. What's more,' he added, sneezing, and taking an enormous handkerchief out of his jacket pocket, 'what's more, I've caught Mrs Strettle's cold. My nose is running like a leaking tap.'

'You've come at just the right moment,' said Dolly. 'Emma, show him the letter! We've had another of them.'

The vet took the sheet of paper in his fingertips. 'Yes, to be sure!' he murmured. 'A genuine blackmail letter this time. I've never seen this kind of thing before except on TV. Were you careful about fingerprints?'

'No, we weren't,' said Dolly. 'Don't

bother acting the detective, Knapp. Read that instead. It doesn't sound like a blackmail letter, it's more as if someone had cold feet. No, the first blackmail letter looks quite different. Fetch the wretched thing, Emma, will you? It's on the table in the living room.'

When Emma stood up, Shaggy trotted expectantly along behind her.

'Forget it, fatso,' said Emma. 'This isn't about food, it's about your friends. Or haven't you even noticed that they're missing yet?'

'Good heavens,' said Knapp when he had read the first letter. 'This is really unpleasant. Emma, is there any coffee left for me? I only want one if you brewed it, mind.'

Emma grinned and brought him a mug.

Knapp looked at the two letters and sneezed into his handkerchief. 'I don't suppose you want to go to the police?'

Dolly shook her head. 'Would you?'

'No.' Knapp sighed. 'Particularly not after this second letter. But you two can't possibly go off there on your own tonight.'

'Oh, don't be silly, Knapp.' Dolly gave Shaggy the end of her breakfast roll. 'Of course I'm going alone. And I was hoping to leave Emma with you.'

'What?' Emma jumped up from her chair. 'Not likely! After all, this is about my horse. I'm coming with you.'

But Knapp let her down. 'I don't think that's a good idea, Emma,' he said, rubbing his red nose. 'It could be dangerous.'

'Anyway, someone has to keep an eye on Mississippi,' said Dolly. 'We're not going to argue about this. You stay here. Knapp, can you stay here yourself tonight? I don't want Emma to be in the place on her own.'

'That's no problem,' said the vet. 'So long as you don't expect me to sleep on your sofa. Only about half of me would fit on it.'

'You can have my bed,' said Dolly. 'It's huge. Then I'll sleep in the spare room when I get back, and Emma sleeps in the stable anyway.'

'I see,' said Knapp.

Emma said nothing at all. She was

furious. Really furious.

'Don't look at me like that,' said Dolly. 'I can't take you with me. If your parents knew what's going on here they'd come and take you home on the spot.'

'Okay, okay,' growled Emma. She angrily pushed her chair back. 'I'm going out to see Mississippi. At least she doesn't tell me what I can and can't do.'

Emma sulked for the rest of the day. She went out into the wood with Mississippi, walking until she was footsore. Then she mucked out the stable, cleaned the tack, changed the water in the outside trough and sat in the sun in front of the paddock fence with the white cat. She didn't put in an appearance at the house at all, except for going in for a little while at lunch to nibble at one of Dolly's oversalted baked potatoes.

Dolly looked at her with a worried expression. 'Don't you like it?' she asked. 'Or are you still feeling offended?'

'Both,' said Emma.

'But darling,' said Dolly, leaning over the table and pinching her cheek, 'can't you try to see it my way? I can't simply drag you off to a meeting like that in the middle of the night.'

'Rubbish!' said Emma. She pushed her plate away and went out again.

When Leo and Max came over they saw what was wrong with her at once.

'What's gone and upset you?' asked Max, mocking her. 'Did Mississippi kick you?'

'Don't be silly!' growled Emma, and she sat down under the walnut tree with the two boys. 'You've got no idea what's going on.'

'Well, tell us then,' said Leo.

Emma looked round. No sign of Lizzie Dockfoot anywhere, and an engine was running in the car repair shop.

'You won't tell anyone?'

'We'll be silent as two graves,' said Max. 'After the gravedigger's filled them in.'

Emma lowered her voice. 'We're being blackmailed.'

The boys looked at her

160

incredulously.

'Wait here.' Emma ran into the house and fetched the letters.

'They stole Dolly's dogs?' cried Max when he had read the first one.

Leo quickly put his hand over his brother's mouth. 'Are you stupid or what?' he hissed angrily. 'You know what big ears Lizzie Dockfoot has.'

He looked at Emma, worried.

'That first letter is horrible,' he said, 'but what about the second?'

Emma shrugged her shoulders. 'That's what I'm so cross about. Of course I wanted to go to the secret meeting tonight, but Dolly says it's too dangerous. And after all, this is about my horse!'

'It could be a trap,' whispered Max.

'I don't think so,' said Leo. 'It's the horse that the Alligator wants, not Dolly.'

Emma leaned back. 'Is Harry back at work again?' she asked. 'Maybe he knows something.'

Max shook his head. 'Leo and I asked after him yesterday. But he's disappeared completely since that time we met the Alligator. Procter doesn't know where he is either.'

Suddenly Leo got up and went over to Dolly's old estate car. He peered through the window, opened the boot, looked at the space inside, and closed it again.

'What does he think he's doing?' Max giggled. 'Leo's sometimes a bit weird! Hey, Leo,' he called. 'Never seen a car before?'

Leo didn't even turn to look at him.

Emma frowned. Then she suddenly smiled.

She quickly looked up at the house, but there was no sign of Dolly. She was usually sitting in the living room at this time of day, drinking tea and listening to the radio. All the better.

Emma left Max sitting there and went over to Leo.

'Will it work?' she asked.

Leo nodded. 'No problem,' he said. 'What with all the mess in there she'll never notice a thing.'

'She'll take Shaggy with her,' said Emma. 'But he always lies on the back seat.'

'What are you two whispering about?' called Max. Suspicious, he came closer.

'A secret,' said Emma. 'See if you can't work it out for yourself.'

Max narrowed his eyes. He looked first at his brother, then at the car, then at Emma.

'Trying to fool me, are you?'

'Not at all,' said Emma. 'Just running a little test to see how slow on the uptake you are.' She giggled. '"Very slow" seems to be the answer.'

'Emma!' Dolly suddenly called from the house. 'Will you go and buy us some cake, or are you still cross?'

'It's okay, I'm fine,' Emma called back. 'I'll go and get the cake.'

'Wonderful! Catch!' Dolly threw her wallet out of the kitchen window.

Max was still standing there staring at the car.

Suddenly he struck his forehead. 'I get it!' he cried. 'You're going to—'

But Leo put his hand over Max's mouth just in time.

CHAPTER 17

Dolly was sitting with the vet in the kitchen when Emma came downstairs in her nightie with a blanket under her arm. It was just ten o'clock.

Emma put her head round the door and yawned. 'I'm going to catch up with my sleep,' she said. 'Good night.'

Dolly looked at her in surprise. 'I'll wake you as soon as I get back, shall I?'

'Fine,' said Emma. 'Don't forget your mace spray.'

'I'll make sure myself that she takes it,' said Knapp. 'Sleep well, Emma.'

*   *   *

It was cool outside, although it had been a hot day. Emma closed the stable door behind her and pushed the tack-cleaning bucket in front of it, just to be on the safe side. Dolly had looked just a tiny bit suspicious.

She didn't put on the light because of the horses. They both became alert anyway when they heard Emma. She went to the boxes, patted the two of them for a while and gave each of them a carrot to nibble. Then she unrolled the blanket she had brought with her. A sweatshirt, a pair of jeans and a pair of socks fell out. She quickly put them on over her nightie, pushed the tack-cleaning bucket back into its proper place, and got under her covers. She set the alarm clock on the straw bale beside her pillow for twelve-thirty.

When Dolly came in an hour later Emma wasn't asleep yet, but she closed her eyes tightly and tried to breathe very slowly and peacefully. Like someone fast asleep. Dolly came back twice, and each time Emma managed to convince her that she was asleep.

When the alarm clock went off at twelve-thirty, she rolled up the extra blanket and put it under her covers so that it would look as if she were still lying under them. To make the whole thing look even more real, she had cropped a little hair from Aldo and Mississippi's tails that afternoon. The horsehair was the same colour as

Emma's hair, and Dolly would never notice the difference in the dark.

Emma arranged the strands of hair on her pillow so that it looked as if she had pulled the covers up over her head. She often did that in her sleep anyway, so she was sure that Dolly wouldn't suspect anything.

It was twenty to one when Emma stole out of the stable. An owl hooted in the distance, and two of the cats were scurrying across the dark yard.

Luckily Dolly never locked her car when she left it in the yard. Emma looked at the house. She could see Dolly's shadow behind the lighted kitchen window. She'd be coming out any minute now.

Emma opened the hatchback, pushed aside a couple of the old dog blankets that Dolly always kept in the car—and almost bit her tongue with fright.

Something was moving under the blankets.

'Quick!' whispered Leo, pulling her down. 'Close the boot.'

Emma did as he said, and pulled one

of the blankets over her.

'Are you crazy?' she whispered. 'What are you doing here?'

'Coming with you, what do you think?'

'What about your parents?'

'They've been asleep for ages. Bakers have to get up at three in the morning.'

'And Max?' Emma heard the house door close, and footsteps approached.

'Max is asleep as well,' whispered Leo. 'Now keep quiet or she'll find us.'

But Dolly went past the car. She was probably going to take a last look inside the stable.

'What do we do if she notices you're not in there?' Leo whispered.

'She won't,' Emma replied.

At that moment Dolly came back. She opened the back door of the car and called to Shaggy, 'We're off. Jump in, fatso.' The car rocked as Shaggy jumped up on the back seat. Two empty bottles rolled against Emma. She heard loud snuffling sounds above her head.

'Shaggy!' said Dolly. 'Lie down.

There are no dog biscuits left in the back.'

Then she started the engine and drove off.

Dolly's style of driving was enough to shake up a passenger in the seat next to her, but that was nothing compared to this journey. Emma and Leo felt as if they were being shaken to bits. After a while it got even worse. They must be going along the stony path that led through the woods to the old fishermen's hut.

The big car jolted over the stones as if it were driving over a bed of nails, but all the same Dolly didn't slow down. Emma and Leo slid about on the floor of the boot like a couple of old rolls of carpet. Then at last Dolly stopped.

When she switched off the engine all was suddenly perfectly quiet. Quiet and pitch dark.

Another owl hooted somewhere. Emma and Leo peered out from under their blankets. Dolly opened the driver's door, and the light inside the car came on.

'Here we go, Shaggy,' Emma heard her grandmother say. 'Not afraid of the dark all of a sudden, are you?'

Shaggy jumped up, put his big head over the top of the back seat and nosed frantically at the blanket with Emma lying under it.

'Oh, for goodness' sake, fatso!' Dolly scolded him. 'Can't you take your mind off food just for once?'

At that very moment Emma felt a sneeze coming.

A great big sneeze.

Next minute Dolly was pulling the blanket off her face. 'Emma!' she cried, horrified. 'Heavens above!'

Sniffing, Emma sat up. 'Well, I had to keep an eye on you,' she said.

'Me too!' said Leo, emerging from under his blanket like a ghost.

Dolly groaned, while Shaggy licked the children's faces.

'You two stay here!' she said. 'Right here in the car. Or I'll feed you to the chickens first thing in the morning, understand?'

Emma and Leo nodded.

Dolly pulled Shaggy off the back seat

and slammed the door. Cautiously, Emma and Leo sat up and peered over the back of the seat. Dolly had left the car headlights switched on. Their light fell on the fishermen's hut. There was a light on inside it too.

Emma saw her grandmother and Shaggy going up to the closed door.

'Come on!' she whispered to Leo. 'It makes no difference now, she's cross already.'

They pushed the boot open and crept out of the car like a couple of cats.

'Now what?' asked Leo quietly.

Dolly had already reached the hut. She was just raising her hand to knock on the door when it opened.

Harry came out.

And Tom and Jerry came with him. Barking and wagging their tails, they jumped up at Dolly, licked her hands and face, and then started racing around in the little clearing with Shaggy as if they hadn't seen each other for years.

Harry just stood there looking at his feet, saying nothing.

'Come *on*.' Emma nudged Leo.

They ran past the playful dogs and up to Dolly. Dolly did give them a stern look, but she didn't send them back to the car.

'Hello, Harry!' said Leo.

Harry raised his head and looked at him. 'Oh, so it's you again!' he muttered. 'Where's your brother? Don't you take him around with you any more these days?'

'He's asleep,' said Leo. 'And what are *you* doing here? Did you steal the dogs?'

Harry scratched the back of his neck. 'It wasn't difficult. They jumped into my car of their own accord.'

'I'm inclined to believe you,' said Dolly. 'I've always told that precious pair that their passion for cars would get them into trouble. But what about the letter? You know the one I mean, the really nasty typewritten one. Did you write that as well?'

'No.' Harry leaned in the doorway of the hut and dug his hands in his trouser pockets. 'I didn't. I mean, something like that wouldn't even occur to me.'

171

'But you did put it in my letter box, didn't you?' Dolly looked at him intently.

Harry nodded.

'You don't have to tell me on whose instructions,' said Dolly. 'We all know the answer to that. But *why* did you do it? That really does interest me.'

Emma was watching Harry, who didn't know where to look.

'That devil knows something about me,' he muttered.

'Knows what about you?' asked Dolly.

'I've been nicking spare parts from Procter. Gosling threatened to tell him.'

'Good heavens, Harry!' cried Dolly. 'Procter's known about those spare parts for ages. But he likes you, so he didn't say anything about it. People don't go along with blackmail over a thing like that. They don't go kidnapping two nice dogs for that sort of reason.'

'Well, I didn't go along with it in the end, did I?' said Harry. 'That's why I wrote you the other letter, because I *don't* do things like that. I didn't think it was so bad about that silly piece of paper with the sale agreement on it. Specially because that old nag threw me into the village pond once. But this bad business with the dogs—nope.'

He shook his head.

'Come along.' Dolly took his arm. 'I'll take you home now. You still live with your mother, don't you?'

Harry nodded. 'But I don't want you telling her—'

'I'm not going to tell her,' Dolly interrupted him. 'Or anyone else. The dogs went missing and you found them. That's our story. Emma and Leo will say the same. Right?'

Emma and Leo nodded.

'Of course. In a way, you've sort of saved my horse,' said Emma. 'If the Alligator had kidnapped the dogs himself, I'm sure we'd never have got them back until he had her.'

Harry stared at her in surprise. 'Well, nice of you to see it that way,' he murmured. 'But who on earth is the Alligator?'

CHAPTER 18

It was almost three by the time Dolly turned off the car engine again, back at her house. The moon was still in the sky, but the night was not quite so black now.

Tom and Jerry raced cheerfully across the yard, scaring the cats away from mouse-holes and barking so noisily that Lizzie Dockfoot threw a slipper out of her bedroom window. Jerry took it straight to the place where he hid his bones and buried it.

'Tired?' Dolly put an arm around Emma's shoulders.

Emma nodded.

They went over to the stable together.

'He can't take Mississippi away from me now, can he?' asked Emma.

Dolly shook her head. 'No, but I tell you what. We ought to go there all the same. To Clipperbush's farm, I mean. Teach him a lesson. One he won't forget in a hurry. But we can discuss that in the morning when our heads are clear.'

'Let's do that.' Emma yawned and opened the stable door. Shaggy, Tom and Jerry pushed past her legs and flung themselves down in the straw.

'Well, you have plenty of company now.' Dolly dropped a kiss on Emma's cheek. 'Sleep well. And thanks for wanting to protect me. That was really nice of you and Leo. And brave. Stupid, but brave. Good night.'

'Good night,' said Emma. She watched Dolly walking back to the house. Two cats scurried after her and slipped indoors too.

Emma closed the stable door and walked over the rustling straw to Mississippi.

'Everything's all right now,' she whispered. 'You don't need to worry any more.'

Then she crawled under her blanket. She just managed to get her shoes off before she fell asleep. With three dogs' heads on her stomach.

*   *   *

When she woke up again the sun was shining into the stable. Mississippi and Aldo were impatiently kicking the walls of their boxes, and the three dogs were looking for mice in the straw. Emma took the alarm clock out from under her pillow and groaned. Ten o'clock! She'd overslept. And how!

She quickly put her shoes on, went to the feed box and mixed them some cubes and chaff. Then she fetched fresh water, and when the horses had fed she took them out into the paddock. She herself went over to the house. Dolly and Mr Knapp were still sitting over their breakfasts in the kitchen.

'Did you oversleep too?' asked Dolly. 'If my tabby cat hadn't started licking my chin this morning I'd still be snoring away in your bed. And Knapp here,' she said, patting the vet on the back, 'has written himself a sick note.'

'That's right,' said Knapp with his mouth full. 'How your grandmother can sleep in that bed is a mystery to me. If only I'd opted for the sofa! My

176

back feels as if a herd of elephants had been dancing on it last night. I couldn't even take a budgie out of its cage and put it on the examination table today.'

'Well, I feel wonderful.' Emma poured dry food into the dogs' bowls and put a little milk on it for each of them. Then she helped herself to a roll and a glass of milk and sat down at the table beside Knapp.

'Yes, I heard about your secret commando raid,' he said. 'And about Harry the sorry dognapper. All I can't work out is what you're going to do about the Alligator now.'

'Dolly wants to go there,' said Emma, taking a bite of her roll. The white cat jumped on her lap, licked her whiskers and purred. She had grown quite plump in the last few days. Dolly had probably been right—there would soon be a litter of kittens.

'Well, well!' Knapp looked sideways at Dolly, rather concerned. 'So you want to go there. At your age! Taking on a criminal who thinks nothing of breaking and entering.' He shook his head. 'If you ask me, you ought to leave the rest of this to the police. You can be glad that Harry defused the whole thing. Just leave the Alligator to his fate. He's back again, by the way. Leo's mother saw his car. She told me so when I went to buy the rolls this morning.'

'Well, of course he's back,' said Dolly. 'He expects to take delivery of Mississippi.' She laughed. 'Oh, Knapp, how I look forward to seeing the expression on his stupid face. I'm not about to miss the chance of that. The police? No, I'd like to teach Gosling a lesson myself. And I already have a plan. I'll take Emma with me this time. If I don't she'll only go smuggling herself into my car again.'

'Exactly,' said Emma.

'And of course,' said Dolly, pouring the vet another coffee, 'you come into my plan as well.'

'Me?' cried Knapp in alarm.

'Yes, you,' said Dolly. 'You still have that neat little dictaphone?'

Knapp frowned. 'What are you going to do with that?'

'I'll tell you in a minute,' said Dolly.

'We need a trailer as well. Can you get hold of one for us? By, let's say, four o'clock this afternoon?'

'Of course,' said Knapp. 'But—'

'No buts,' said Dolly. 'You want the man to get his just deserts too, don't you?'

'Of course.' Knapp sighed.

'There, you see?' Dolly shooed the white cat off the table and leaned back. 'Then listen carefully. Here's my plan . . .'

CHAPTER 19

The blackmail letter had said six o'clock.

All the preparations for Dolly's plan were completed by five-thirty sharp.

Max and Leo were standing at the gate, and looked left out when Shaggy jumped into the car first.

'You're not really going to give him Mississippi, are you?' asked Leo.

'Of course not,' said Emma. 'Take good care of Tom and Jerry.'

'We will.' Max bit his lip. 'Oh, go on, tell us what you're planning.'

'No time.' Emma waved to the pair of them and climbed into the passenger seat. 'We'll tell you all about it when we get back.'

'Why can't we come too?' complained Max. 'You're being mean. We could hide, couldn't we? You wouldn't believe how small we can make ourselves, Dolly.'

'No,' said Dolly, getting into the car. 'Your father would never sell me a nice fresh roll again if I took you with me.' She looked at Emma. 'Ready to go?'

Emma nodded. Her heart was in her mouth.

Shaggy was licking his paws noisily on the back seat.

'We'll show that villain,' said Dolly. Then she started the engine and carefully drove out of the gate.

'Where are you taking that horse, Dolly?' asked Lizzie Dockfoot as the trailer passed her.

'You'll find out soon enough, Lizzie!' Dolly called back. 'Tomorrow at the latest. Then you'll all have something

180

to gossip about. Enough to last you for weeks—no, months!'

And she and Emma drove out of the village.

*　　　*　　　*

The Alligator was already waiting for them, leaning against his car with a self-satisfied smile.

'Just you wait!' murmured Dolly as she drove up to him. 'That grin will soon be wiped off your face.'

She braked so close to the Alligator's car that he flung up his hands in alarm.

'Hey, what's the idea?' he cried. 'Watch out for my car, can't you?'

Dolly and Emma climbed out and opened the back door of their own car. With one bound, Shaggy jumped out. He raised his nose, sniffing.

'Stop, stop! Shut that dog in again,' said the Alligator. 'Who said you were to bring it with you?'

'The dog needs to wee,' replied Dolly. 'Are you going to tell him not to? I wouldn't try it myself.'

Shaggy trotted across the yard,

sniffing at every stone, with the Alligator watching him in annoyance.

'You're afraid of dogs, aren't you?' said Emma. 'Shaggy isn't dangerous. He only plays up with people he doesn't like. He can be quite nasty then. But you're such a nice person. Kidnapping his friends and threatening to kill them. I'm sure he must like you. Don't you, Shaggy?'

The big dog looked at her, wagged his tail and went on sniffing his way over the yard of the Clipperbush farm.

'Very funny,' growled the Alligator. 'What do you want? Wouldn't you be better off at home?'

Emma looked at him darkly.

'The horse belongs to me, doesn't she?' she snapped.

'Not for much longer.' Albert Gosling had his self-satisfied smile back. 'But do you know what? I'm generous. You can take her to my stable. Then I won't have to get my shoes dirty.'

'Just a moment.' Dolly put her arm round Emma's shoulders. 'We're not done yet, not by a long way. How do I know my dogs are all right? How do I know you haven't sent them to the happy hunting grounds in the sky by now?'

The Alligator took a step towards Dolly. 'You've brought all this trouble on yourself just because you were too obstinate to give me back my rightful property. Those are the facts.'

Dolly looked at him, unmoved. 'How are my dogs?' she asked again.

'They're all right!' snorted the Alligator. 'They're fine! Now, get my horse out of that trailer.'

Shaggy trotted up behind him and sniffed his trouser legs. When the Alligator felt the dog's muzzle on the back of his calf he jumped, and stood there as stiff as a board.

'For heaven's sake!' he whispered. 'Shut this wretched dog in your car, will you?'

Dolly grinned.

'Come along, Shaggy,' she said, taking hold of the big dog's collar. 'Someone's afraid of being eaten alive. As if you'd like the taste of a man like that!'

She lowered the car window, bundled Shaggy into the back seat and closed the door behind him.

Relieved, the Alligator leaned against the wing of his car. 'At last!' he said. 'Right, now for the horse.'

'Good heavens above, what a hurry the man is in!' sighed Dolly. 'Wouldn't you like to have your charming letter back first? You don't get to write a genuine blackmail letter every day of the week. You could frame it and hang it over your bed.'

'Very funny.' The Alligator adjusted his tie. 'But you're right. You can give me the letter and the copy of that sale agreement now. Just so that we don't forget about it later.'

'Emma.' Dolly nudged her in the ribs with her elbow. 'Have you got them both?'

Emma nodded.

'I trust you didn't get the silly idea of making another copy?' asked the Alligator. 'That would be very bad luck for your grandmother's dogs.' He put out his hand. 'Right, let's have them.'

Emma put her hand in her jacket

pocket—and then caught her breath in shock.

There was Leo, in the bushes near the stables! When he saw that Gosling's back was turned, he ducked low, scuttled over the yard and disappeared behind the Alligator's car.

'What are you gawping at?' asked the Alligator impatiently. 'Hand over those papers, and look sharp about it.'

'Okay, okay,' muttered Emma. She forced herself not to look at the car. Instead, she fumbled around in her pocket as if she couldn't get the letter and the copy of the agreement out.

When she put the papers into the Alligator's hand, her fingers were shaking slightly. Leo was just opening the driver's door of the car—without the faintest sound.

'At last!' said Gosling. He glanced suspiciously first at the copy of the agreement, then at his letter. Emma cast another quick look at his car. The driver's door was still open, but Leo was nowhere to be seen.

Relieved, Emma looked at Dolly, but

she obviously hadn't noticed Leo. She was taking down the ramp of the trailer.

The Alligator put the papers in the inside pocket of his jacket. 'Can't you get a move on?' he snapped at Dolly.

Dolly climbed into the trailer—and led out Aldo. The Alligator's eyes almost popped out of his head.

'What's the big idea?' he yelled. 'Are you trying to make fun of me? That's not Mississippi.'

'Oh, really?' Dolly patted the gelding's neck. 'Well, Gosling, I have to admit we *have* in fact been making fun of you all the time. Give me the tape, would you, Emma?'

'Tape?' The Alligator barred Emma's way, grabbed her roughly and pulled her jacket open. Knapp's dictaphone was fixed to her sweater with sticky tape. It was still running.

'Let go of me!' Emma tried to struggle free, but Gosling was holding her firmly. He tore the dictaphone free and flung it on the ground.

'You'll be sorry for this!' he shouted at Dolly. 'I'll make mincemeat of your dogs.'

'We'll make mincemeat of *you*!' yelled Max. Shouting at the top of his voice, he stormed out from behind the Alligator's car. Leo arrived from the other side of it.

Both boys ran at the Alligator, grabbed his legs and knocked him off his feet.

Shouting with rage, he landed in the dirt. The dictaphone flew out of his hand and landed at Emma's feet. She snatched it up and ran over to Dolly, who was having a lot of difficulty holding the agitated Aldo.

Emma looked round. Max and Leo were sitting on the Alligator, pushing his flailing arms and legs down on the paving stones.

'Can you keep him there another moment?' asked Dolly.

'You bet!' said Max. 'It'll be a real pleasure.'

'I'm going to wring those dogs' necks!' bellowed the Alligator.

Dolly went over to him and looked down with a smirk. 'Shall I tell you something? You don't even have my dogs any more, you idiot. Harry gave them back to me some time ago.'

That deprived the Alligator of speech for a moment or so. But he soon recovered.

'So what?' he shouted. 'That audiotape won't do you any good. The courts don't recognize such things. And if you were thinking of calling those snotty-nosed boys as witnesses, you can forget that too!'

'Yes, I know.' Dolly went over to her car, opened the boot and pushed the dog blankets aside.

'Right, Knapp,' she said, 'did you hear all that?'

Groaning, his hair untidy, the vet swung his long legs out of the boot space. 'Good heavens, Dolly,' he said. 'I wouldn't do a thing like this for anyone but you. I don't suppose I'll ever get my legs straightened out again.'

'And we know how much we owe you, dear friend.' Dolly led him over to the place where the Alligator was lying flat on the paving stones. 'May I introduce you? This is Mr Aaron

Knapp, veterinary surgeon by profession, and most certainly a witness who'll be welcomed by the court.'

'A witness who heard every word of what's been said,' added Knapp. 'Thanks to his excellent hearing and the open car window.'

The Alligator groaned and closed his eyes. He had run out of anything else to say.

'Let him up, boys,' said Dolly.

'Wouldn't it be better if we stayed sitting on him until he's arrested?' asked Leo.

Dolly shook her head. 'That won't be necessary. We're all going to the police station now. We'll make our statements, and then they'll be paying a call on this charming character very soon.'

'Oh, all right.' Reluctantly, the boys let go of their captive.

The Alligator scrambled to his feet, brushed the dirt off his suit and went to his car without another word.

When he got in, Max and Leo nudged Emma and grinned.

'Where are my car keys?' growled the Alligator through the window of the passenger seat.

'Here.' Leo put his hand in his jeans pocket and brought out the keys. 'But you must say "please", or they'll end up on the muck heap.'

'Please.' The Alligator spat the word out venomously.

'Okay, I'm not as nasty as you think,' said Leo, throwing the keys in through the car window.

With squealing tyres, the Alligator drove out of the yard.

Dolly, Emma and Knapp grinned at each other.

'How did we do?' asked Dolly.

'It was brilliant,' said Emma. 'Absolutely brilliant. And these two,' she added, nudging Max and Leo, 'weren't so bad either, were they?'

'Oh, well,' said Leo, shrugged his shoulders, 'it was just a pity we had to let the Alligator go.'

'Why? What were you planning to do with him?' asked Knapp, interested.

'Maybe tie him to that tree, for instance,' said Leo.

'Hoping for rain,' added Leo.

'Yes.' Dolly grinned. 'I'd have enjoyed that too. But we're nice people, aren't we?'

'Very nice,' said Knapp. 'And that's why you're going to drive me home now. I urgently need a hot bath.'

'No problem.' Dolly reached through the open car window and petted Shaggy's head. 'How about you two snotty-nosed boys?'

'We left our bikes back in the bushes there,' said Max.

'Well, I'm going to ride home.' Emma went over to Aldo and patted his neck reassuringly. 'Okay? I'm sure you'd like that better than going back in that tin can.'

'All right.' Dolly gave Emma Aldo's halter and got into the car. 'Then I hereby declare Operation Alligator successfully concluded.'

CHAPTER 20

Emma gave Mississippi a huge bunch of carrots to eat in honour of the day, and tied pink bows into her mane. When Emma took the ribbons out of Clipperbush's saddlebag, the mare got quite excited. She kept nudging Emma with her nose, scraping her hoof in the straw and snorting. She's probably remembering Clipperbush, thought Emma, and she quickly put the saddlebag away again.

She brushed Missie's mane. The mare usually liked that, but this time she just shifted restlessly from one leg to the other. She didn't calm down until Emma took her out into the paddock to join Aldo.

First the gelding snuffled at Mississippi's bows for some time, and then, as she grazed beside him, he patiently pulled them out of her mane with his teeth.

'Looks as if Aldo thinks she's prettier without bows, doesn't it?' said

Emma. She and Dolly were leaning on the paddock fence.

'Looks like it,' Dolly agreed, and she smiled.

Emma sighed happily. She squinted into the evening sun hanging low above the trees. 'Now *really* no one can take her away from me,' she murmured.

'That's right.' Dolly plucked a snail off the fence and put it down in the grass. 'Although I did have my doubts until yesterday.'

'Why?' Emma looked at her grandmother in alarm.

Dolly tugged at her earlobe. 'Well, officially, Gosling wasn't yet Clipperbush's heir when he sold us Mississippi. And since selling her meant he would never be his heir, was our sale agreement valid? Or had Mississippi belonged to the RSPCA all this time?'

'Oh no!' groaned Emma.

'It's all right!' Dolly smiled. 'I didn't want to worry you unnecessarily, so I asked Knapp to consult a lawyer for us. And the lawyer said that Missie belongs to you now in any case. Happy now?'

'You bet!' sighed Emma. And her heart suddenly stopped thudding so hard.

'You know,' she said, 'Missie seemed very nervous when I was putting those ribbons in her mane. Do you think maybe she doesn't like being prettified like that?'

'Could be!' Dolly looked at the pasture where Mississippi was enjoying herself by rolling in the grass. 'Or maybe she was excited because Clipperbush usually decked her out before they went for a ride together. Who knows, perhaps she'd like to be ridden through the village again?'

'Do you think so?' Emma looked at Mississippi and Aldo. The two horses were standing side by side rubbing their necks together.

Dolly shrugged her shoulders. 'Well, it's possible, isn't it? Maybe you should try it once all this fuss and bother with the will is over. The most important thing in riding is that the horse and its rider get on well with each other. And everyone who understands anything about animals can see that Missie is crazy about you. Just look at the way she's always nibbling your sweater so lovingly.'

Emma laughed. 'You're right,' she said. 'But I really don't want to ride her unless she'd enjoy it too. When do they open that will?'

'In two days' time,' said Dolly. 'And I can't tell you how happy I'll be when all this annoying business is over.'

'Me too,' murmured Emma.

'Coming in now?' asked Dolly. 'It's getting cool. And it will be dark quite soon. We could warm up the rest of that delicious soup you made yesterday.'

Emma nodded. 'Just coming. I'll take the horses back into the stable first.'

The stable was still warm from the afternoon sun. Emma put Aldo and Missie in their boxes, put some feed in their mangers and fished a struggling beetle out of Missie's bucket of water. Then she opened the tack box containing Missie's saddle and bridle, took them out, and cleaned them both thoroughly with saddle soap.

195

As she hung the saddle over the door of the third, empty box, she heard a faint mewing. The white cat was lying in the straw right in the corner of the box. With four tiny kittens suckling milk from her teats.

Very quietly, Emma went closer. 'Oh, kitty,' she whispered, kneeling down beside the cat. 'What pretty little babies. They all look just like you.'

The white cat looked at her and yawned.

'You chose a bad day to have them, though,' said Emma. 'What with the excitement we forgot all about you. I tell you what, I'll get you something to eat and drink. Back in a minute!'

She ran back to the house like lightning. The sky was already getting darker, a strong wind had risen, and the leaves of the big walnut tree rustled as if a huge flock of birds were flying above Emma's head.

Dolly was in the kitchen, with the telephone in one hand, and in the other the wooden spoon she was using to stir the soup. 'Well,' she was saying, 'I must ring off now, or my soup will be

196

spoilt. You can hear the rest of it tomorrow.'

'Dolly,' said Emma, 'the white cat has had her kittens.'

'My goodness!' Dolly took the pan off the stove. 'Kittens as well! How many are there?'

'Four,' said Emma. 'I'm just going to take her something to eat and drink.'

'You do that,' said Dolly. 'But hurry up, or the soup will get cold. My word, what a day!'

*   *   *

When they were finally sitting at the table, the phone rang four times, but Dolly didn't answer it.

'It's been like that ever since I came indoors,' she sighed. 'Leo and Max have been talking about their heroic deeds at home. And then their mother was on the line, asking me if her sons are right round the bend or whether there was a grain of truth in their story. And after that she must have told all her neighbours. So now the story of Operation Alligator has gone all round the entire village, and the nearby villages will know the news tomorrow morning. Kidnapping, blackmail— nothing so exciting has happened around here for at least thirty years.' She laughed. 'I can't wait to find out what else is supposed to have happened overnight. Perhaps we faced a whole gang and there was a shoot-out! But there's a practical outcome to all this. Can you guess what it is?'

Emma shook her head.

'I can ask everyone who calls whether they'd like a sweet little kitten to hunt mice for them,' said Dolly. 'That way at least some good will come of all the gossip. Are you going to sleep in the stable again tonight?'

'Of course,' said Emma. 'It's cosy there. Just in case the Alligator thinks up some other nasty trick. You never know.'

CHAPTER 21

Emma didn't see the Alligator again until the day when the will was read at the District Court in town. He was sitting three places away from her, tight-lipped, in front of the desk for the lawyer who was going to be executor of the will. Mrs Strettle was there as well. She still had a terrible cold. Her dog Barnabas was under her seat, chewing hard at his lead.

'Good morning,' said the lawyer. 'My name is Unwin. You have been invited here for the opening of the last will and testament of John Clipperbush. His housekeeper Mrs Strettle, who registered his death, has been kind enough to give us the names of all those who have been mentioned in the will. For the records of this meeting, I will just make sure you are all here.' He cleared his throat. 'Mr Albert Gosling?'

The Alligator nodded with a dark expression.

'Mrs Dora Strettle?'

'Here!' Mrs Strettle put up her hand like a schoolgirl in class. 'That's me.'

'And Mrs Dolores Flowerdew?'

'Present,' said Dolly.

'Good.' Mr Unwin nodded, pleased. 'Then I will now open and read the will of Mr John Clipperbush.' He held up a sealed envelope. 'As you can all see for yourselves, the seal is unbroken.' The lawyer broke it with a practised movement and took out a densely written sheet of paper. He cleared his throat again, looked round at everyone and read:

' "I, John Clipperbush, being in full possession of my mental powers, do hereby leave to my nephew Albert Gosling all my landed property in the village of Anderham, to wit the house and furniture, the stables and the land belonging to the house, as well as my mare Mississippi, but on one condition: he must never sell the horse, and must have Mississippi cared for to the best of his ability until her natural death, which, it is to be hoped, will not be for a long time. If he does not keep the horse, the farm and all its land will go to the RSPCA in Neddlestead."'

Mr Unwin raised his head and looked at Albert Gosling. 'Can you comply with the conditions mentioned?'

'No,' growled the Alligator. 'I can't. But I am going to contest this stupid will. All of you here can be sure of that.'

'Go ahead and contest it,' said Dolly. 'But don't you think you've already made enough of a fool of yourself?'

The Alligator gave Dolly such a black look that Mrs Strettle started giggling nervously.

Mr Unwin cleared his throat. 'I will continue,' he said. 'John Clipperbush writes here: "To my housekeeper Dora Strettle I leave all my cooking pots and pans, my china, most of which she has broken already, all the cleaning materials and the rug in my study, which has been so well chewed by her dog Barnabas."'

Dora Strettle forced a smile and scratched Barnabas on the back of his fat neck.

' "Finally," ' Mr Unwin went on, ' "I leave to my old sweetheart Dolly Flowerdew my favourite book, the most remarkable book ever written, *Tom Sawyer and Huckleberry Finn*. She is the only person who appreciates it properly." '

Mr Unwin folded up Clipperbush's will and put it carefully back in the envelope.

'And what about his stocks and shares?' cried the Alligator. 'What did he do with all his money? It isn't in the house, and the bank doesn't know what happened to it either. Did he bury it somewhere? Did he want it to moulder away underground?'

'I'm sorry,' said Mr Unwin, leaning back in his chair. 'There's no mention of stocks and shares in the will.'

'But he had them!' shouted the Alligator. 'He showed me the certificates for all his stocks and shares. Stacks of them. Where are they? Did he heat his stove with them? Or feed them to that stupid mare of his?'

'Lower your voice a little, please, Mr

Gosling,' said Mr Unwin. 'I do not think anyone in this room is deaf, or wishes to be deafened. Mrs Strettle, Mrs Flowerdew, do you accept the legacies left to you?'

Mrs Strettle, red in the face, nodded.

Dolly smiled. 'Of course,' she said. 'I shall treasure the book. A wonderful opportunity to read it again, although I expect I shall have to take care it doesn't fall apart. John Clipperbush was always reading it.'

'Oh, it's in very good condition,' said Mr Unwin, and he took a fat envelope out of the desk. 'In fact, it is a remarkable copy.'

'I've heard enough of all this. I'm off.' The Alligator pushed his chair back so violently that Barnabas hid behind Mrs Strettle's legs. 'I have better things to do than listen to silly chatter about some old book. My uncle must really have been senile when he made this will.'

Angrily, he made for the door.

'Which will exactly do you mean, Mr Gosling?' called the lawyer after him. 'The fact is, your uncle left two wills.'

The Alligator stopped dead.

Mr Unwin leaned back in his chair with a smile of satisfaction.

Everyone present gaped at him, speechless. Emma's heart had begun beating much too fast again.

'Ah. I see that this information is a surprise to all of you present, am I right?' Mr Unwin held up the envelope containing Clipperbush's will. 'About two weeks after he had made the will that I have just read out,' the lawyer went on, 'John Clipperbush deposited this second will.'

Mr Unwin looked all round the room, and then held up the thick envelope that he had taken out of the desk. 'As you see, the seal on this envelope is also unbroken, as the law requires.'

Unobtrusively, the Alligator went back to his chair. Once again Mr Unwin broke the seal, opened the envelope and put his hand into it.

'For goodness' sake!' Mrs Strettle leaned so far forward that she almost fell off her chair. 'Don't keep us in suspense like this!'

'Why not?' asked Mr Unwin, with a friendly smile for her. 'The deceased obviously liked the idea of a little suspense, don't you agree?' He looked at Emma. 'What do you think is inside this envelope, young lady?' he asked her.

'No idea!' said Emma.

Mr Unwin took a book out of the envelope.

'This is John Clipperbush's copy of *Tom Sawyer*,' he announced. 'Mrs Flowerdew's legacy.'

'I wish I knew what was going on!' groaned Mrs Strettle.

'Hold your tongue!' the Alligator snapped, looking at Mr Unwin. 'Yes, the book. What about it?'

Mr Unwin leaned over his desk and handed the book to Emma. 'I take it that you are Mrs Flowerdew's granddaughter, so may I ask you to open this book at the first page?'

Emma did as he said.

'Something's been written on the page,' she said, surprised. 'Handwritten. But it's rather scrawly writing. I can't read it.'

205

Inquisitively, Mrs Strettle peered over Emma's shoulder. As for the Alligator, he was shifting restlessly about on his chair.

Only Dolly sat perfectly still.

'Oh, Clipperbush, Clipperbush,' she murmured. 'What have you thought up this time?'

Emma gave the book back to Mr Unwin.

He cleared his throat, looked at Emma with a twinkle in his eye, and read:

' "I, John Clipperbush, being in full possession of my mental powers, such as they still are, do hereby leave to Dolly Flowerdew my house in America. Although she did not want to go and live with me there, perhaps she will like the house when I am dead. After all, Dolly was always fond of adventures. Signed, John Clipperbush." '

'I don't understand this at all!' The Alligator jumped up as if he had been stung by a tarantula. 'So that's where his money is! He spent it in America. Oh, fabulous!' Snorting with rage, he made for Dolly. 'First you cheat me out of my inheritance, then you get most of it left to you!'

'You leave my grandmother alone!' cried Emma, barring his way. 'You nasty, horrible man—you Alligator!'

And she kicked him in the shin. Quite hard.

The Alligator landed on Mrs Strettle's lap.

Mrs Strettle began screaming blue murder. Barnabas jumped out from under her chair and bit the Alligator's left shoe.

'Quiet!' cried Mr Unwin. 'I will have quiet!'

When none of them heard him, he banged the *Tom Sawyer* book down on his desk, but even that didn't work.

Then Dolly stood up, prised the growling Barnabas off the Alligator's shoe, hauled the Alligator off Mrs Strettle's lap by his tie and put her hand over Mrs Strettle's mouth.

Suddenly there was peace and quiet.

'Mr Unwin,' said Dolly. 'Can you tell me whereabouts in America Mr Clipperbush's house is?'

'Yes, of course,' said Mr Unwin. 'On

the Upper Mississippi. I'm afraid I can't pronounce the name of the place, but I'll write down the address for you.'

'Please do that,' said Dolly, taking Emma's hand. 'Emma, let's go home. Shaggy will have eaten half the living-room rug by now.' She picked up the *Tom Sawyer* book. 'May I take this with me?'

'Just a moment.' Mr Unwin took out a pair of scissors. 'If you have no objection.' He carefully cut out the title page with Clipperbush's second will written on it. 'This has to stay in the hands of the District Court, as an official document, so to speak. Do you understand?'

'Of course,' said Dolly. 'So long as you don't cut any of the story out. I especially like the beginning.'

CHAPTER 22

'In America?' Max was green with envy.

'Wow, we've never inherited anything in America. We've never even been there.'

Max and Leo were sitting on a sack of oats in the stable, watching Emma making Mississippi look pretty.

'Nor have I,' said Emma, rummaging around in Clipperbush's old saddlebag. 'I'm sure there was another little bell somewhere here.'

Aldo watched suspiciously from his box. He kicked its wooden wall impatiently.

'Yes, all right,' murmured Emma. 'You can both go out in a moment. Missie is nearly ready.'

'Why are you dolling her up like that?' asked Max.

Emma closed the saddlebag and hung it back on its hook. 'Because I'm going to ride her today,' she said. 'I'm going to ride Missie through the village, the way old Mr Clipperbush used to.'

She went over to the crate with the tack in it, took out the bridle, the attractive saddle-cloth and the saddle, and went back to Missie with them. Emma knew exactly how to saddle a horse. Dolly had taught her with Aldo, although she always rode him bareback.

Mississippi stood perfectly still when Emma put the saddle-cloth on her back. 'Happy?' asked Emma softly. She put Clipperbush's saddle on the mare's back, and tightened the girth. Missie was still perfectly calm.

'You're crazy,' muttered Max. 'She won't let anyone ride her.'

'Oh no?' Emma put the bridle on Missie and a halter on Aldo. 'Just because she threw that idiot Harry off? You can't blame her for that.'

She clicked her tongue and led the two horses past the boys and out into the open air.

'Come on,' said Max, making his brother follow him. 'We have to see this.'

It was a beautiful day. The sun was shining, and a warm wind blew through the trees. Dolly's cats were lying stretched out on the warm stones, the chickens were scratching in the sand, and Tom and Jerry lay in the shade, panting.

'Does Dolly know you're going to ride Missie?' asked Max.

'No, she doesn't,' replied Emma. 'She's playing cards with her friends at Henrietta's place. But I know she'd let me.'

She opened the gate to the paddock with a jolt, tied Missie to the fence and took Aldo's halter off. 'There you go,' she said, giving him a slap on his flank. 'You can have the day off.'

Missie pricked up her ears, chewed at the bit and looked at Emma. She trod restlessly from hoof to hoof.

'They'll all be amazed, won't they?' Emma whispered to her.

'Dolly wouldn't let you!' Max climbed up on the fence. 'She definitely wouldn't. I bet you fly thirty feet through the air and land in Lizzie's rose beds.'

'Well, I bet Emma will do it,' said Leo.

He went over to Missie and stroked her nose.

'You're only saying that because you're in love with Emma!' Max called down from the fence.

Leo made a face at him. Then he looked at Emma, embarrassed, but she acted as if she hadn't heard. She stroked Mississippi's neck, brushed a fly off her nose and straightened the ribbon bows.

'She looks lovely, doesn't she?' said Emma softly. 'In spite of the white stripes.'

Leo nodded. 'Kind of like an American Indian horse.'

Emma smiled at him.

'When do you start?' called Max, balancing on the old fence as if he were riding a buffalo.

'What are we betting?' asked Emma. 'What do you bet I'll do it?'

Max grinned. 'I get a kiss if she throws you off.'

'Who from?' asked Emma sarcastically. 'Missie?'

'No, you, of course.'

Emma shrugged her shoulders. 'Okay. And suppose I don't come off?'

'Then Leo gets one,' said Max. 'He's mad keen for one anyway.'

Leo, furious, took a step towards him. 'Stop that, will you? You're an idiot.'

'I know!' said Max. 'But I'll get my kiss, all the same.'

'You won't.' Emma drew Leo closer. 'Look, don't get upset,' she whispered. 'I'll do it all right, and he'll be surprised. Hold Missie for me, will you?'

Leo nodded. He untied Mississippi's bridle from the fence, led her a few paces out into the pasture, and stood there with her.

'Well, Missie,' said Emma, putting her hand on the saddle. 'How about it? Do you feel like a little ride through the village?'

The mare twitched her ears, snorted, and looked at her.

'She's perfectly calm,' said Leo.

Emma patted Missie on the neck again, and then carefully put one foot in the stirrup. Missie turned her head to Emma, interested, but she stood perfectly still.

Emma took a deep breath—and swung herself into the saddle.

Mississippi took a short step back, shook her mane so that Clipperbush's little bells rang, and nudged Leo with her nose.

'Whoaa!' he said, throwing the reins up to Emma. 'I think she's telling you yes, she would like a ride.'

Emma cautiously took the reins, pressed her thighs against Mississippi's flanks, and guided her towards the paddock gate.

The mare walked at her leisure over the short grass, past Max, whose jaw was dropping, past Shaggy, who lay sleeping outside the gate, and out on to the village street.

'Good heavens above!' Lizzie Dockfoot had such a shock when she saw Emma that she dropped her hedge clippers. Her radio was standing on the garden wall, as usual, booming at such high volume that you could hear it in Procter's car repair shop. Mississippi shied and didn't want to go on.

'Take it easy, Missie, take it easy!' said Emma, holding the reins a little more firmly, and using the gentle pressure of her thighs, she guided the mare past Mrs Dockfoot and her radio. Then she turned Missie into the narrow road leading to the village pond.

Emma didn't have to do much. The mare trotted the way that Clipperbush had always ridden her: once round the village pond, past the bakery run by Max and Leo's parents, on to the bus stop and the yards beside the village street.

Mississippi's hooves clattered on the uneven asphalt. Emma felt wonderful, better than ever before in her life. She looked up at the white clouds drifting over the sky and imagined herself somewhere different, in a huge, wild country through which she and Mississippi could ride for days without meeting another soul.

A barking dog jolted Emma out of her dreams.

Legs apart, not much bigger than a

rabbit, it was standing in the middle of the road yapping for all it was worth. Missie shied and refused to move past the little monster.

Emma knew this dog. It belonged to fat Henrietta's son-in-law and barked at everyone who came near his farm. Emma was truly astonished that Henrietta's shop was always full, in spite of the dog.

'Shut up, Zoppo,' she said, throwing the little dog a few biscuits as she guided the restive Missie past him.

Dolly's car was standing behind the farmhouse, where Henrietta had her garden.

Emma rode over to the fence, loosened Mississippi's reins, and let her put her nose down on Henrietta's roses.

Dolly and Henrietta were so deep in their card game that at first they didn't even notice Emma. Only Alma looked up. When she saw Emma on Mississippi's back, she was so surprised that she dropped a biscuit in her sherry.

'Dolly!' she cried. 'Dolly, see that?

Oh!' She put her hands over her eyes. 'Oh, I can't bear to look!'

'Good heavens, Alma!' said Dolly, without looking up from her cards. 'What's the matter now? Has a bumblebee fallen in your sherry?'

Emma grinned. Missie put her neck a little further over the fence, sniffed the rosebuds, and snorted.

Then Dolly and Henrietta also looked up.

'Emma!' cried Dolly. She did look a little alarmed.

'Isn't she rather young to go breaking her neck?' asked Henrietta, pushing a forkful of cake into her mouth.

'Dolly, did you give her permission to do that?' asked Alma, breathless.

Dolly frowned. 'I'm afraid I may actually have put the idea into her head.'

Emma grinned. 'Well, I'll be on my way,' she said. 'Just thought I'd look in and say hello.'

'Don't take her along the main road, will you?' said Dolly, returning to her cards. 'I don't know how Mississippi would react to the cars that race along it.'

'Okay,' said Emma. 'I was only going to take her round the village pond anyway.'

'Here.' Henrietta cut a slice of cake, wrapped it in a paper napkin and handed it to Dolly. 'Be a nice grandmother and give that to your granddaughter. The child must be half starved, what with your cooking skills. But get that horse away from my roses, would you?'

Emma quickly pulled Mississippi back. 'Oh, sorry, Henrietta,' she murmured.

But Henrietta only laughed. 'Never mind, Clipperbush's horse was always crazy about rosebuds. As crazy as her master was about my cakes.'

'You're right,' said Dolly. 'I tell you what, why don't you cut another piece of cake, and Emma can take it to him in honour of the day?'

'What?' asked Emma, baffled. Mississippi was tugging at the reins to get closer to the roses again. 'How do you mean?'

'Well, you could put it on his grave,' said Dolly. 'Instead of flowers.'

'Exactly.' Henrietta cut a large slice of cake and wrapped it in another napkin. 'Clipperbush never could stand flowers anyway.'

'Good gracious me!' groaned Alma. 'What ideas you do get!'

Dolly laughed and handed the two pieces of cake over the fence to Emma.

'Here,' she said. Mississippi turned her neck and sniffed with interest. 'When you ride back you'll pass the church and the graveyard on your way. Clipperbush's grave is the second on the right behind the hedge. There's a horrible sentimental plaster angel on top of it. You can let Mississippi have a bit of a nibble at the rosebushes Mrs Strettle planted.'

'And say who the cake is from!' said Henrietta.

Emma nodded and grinned at her. Alma was still wrinkling her brow disapprovingly.

'Oh, Emma!' Dolly leaned over the fence. 'By the way, do you think your parents would buy you a flight to

America at half-term in the autumn? I don't fancy going to see my house all by myself, but Henrietta would make any plane crash, and Alma gets scared stiff at the mere sight of one.'

Emma reined in Missie and looked incredulously at Dolly. 'America?' she asked.

'I wouldn't want to go to America, not for anything,' said Alma. 'With all those grizzly bears they have there.'

'And the Red Indians!' said Henrietta, laughing at her. 'Don't forget the Red Indians, Alma. Who knows what they might do to you?'

Alma cast her a nasty look.

Emma was staring at Dolly. She seemed to mean it seriously.

'I think flying to America is expensive,' said Emma. 'But if they won't pay for a flight, I'll earn the money myself. I'll do it somehow.'

'You can start tomorrow,' said Henrietta. 'We can always do with someone to help in the shop.'

'Now, now, take it easy,' said Dolly, going back to the table. 'These are really her holidays. Let her go off and take Clipperbush the cake for now.'

And Emma did.

She put the piece of cake down right in front of the angel's feet, while Mississippi nibbled the buds of Mrs Strettle's roses.

'Thank you very much!' she said. 'For everything. Specially for Mississippi. And I'm really, really sorry that you never went to America after all.'